Title page

THOSE WERE THE DAYS by Jo Eliot
-

a novel in 6 parts.

Time present and time past
 Are both perhaps present in time future
And time future contained in time past. .
T.S.Eliot

Sex and drugs and rock and roll are very good indeed
 Ian Drury

It was the best of times,it was the worst of times
Charles Dickens

Chapter One : The Funeral

It was the time of funerals, no longer of aged relatives but of contemporaries. Jane had been to two funerals already that year, one a colleague of Howard's, dead of a heart attack at 63, that had shaken Howard, caused him to cut down on lunches at his club and to at least think about the amount of wine he drank. The funeral of Helen, a friend since the children had been at playgroup 40 years before, had really upset Jane. Poor Helen, she thought of her now as she waited for events to begin. It was ovarian cancer, it seemed so cruel to die before seeing grandchildren grow up. So many funerals but somehow today was different, this was Gideon March's funeral, a man she had once painfully loved. Looking surreptitiously around, past Howard's bulk, she scanned the faces for any she might know. The crematorium was full; she was not the only one craning her neck. She spotted Sarah, and smiled noting that she had grown her hair, was wearing it loosely piled on top of her head. They didn't see each other nearly so often these days, since Sarah had left London, but they kept in touch by phone and email. As she scanned the rows she gave a start of surprise;

"Look Howard, over there, surely that's Leon" she whispered. Claire, Gideon's third wife, had obviously ransacked old address books, made Herculean efforts to contact people from Gideon's past. They had only been married four years; many of those present had never met her before.

"How on earth did she track him down" said Howard,

"Perhaps he saw it in the paper?" speculated Jane.

Gideon had been a successful documentary filmmaker, specialising in social issues and injustice, he had won several awards, including a BAFTA for the film he had made about prisons. His passport into the BBC graduate programme 40 years before had been the documentary he had made on The Summer of Love in California where he had escaped to join Marina after Paul's death. His lengthy obituary in the Guardian had mentioned this and had caused Jane to think back to those awful days. Many of his ex BBC colleagues were here, Jane spotted some familiar faces.

   Sarah had arrived breathless, her train from Bristol had been delayed. She could not face rushing on the tube and then a taxi to the crematorium so had splurged on a taxi all the way to Golders Green. As she sat composing herself she decided it had been a necessary expense. She spotted Howard's bulk half way down the aisle and Jane's sleek dark bob. Jane turned and they exchanged discreet smiles. Like Jane she looked about, what a lot of people. Gideon had always been a charismatic figure, his phenomenal energy, sharp wit and good looks, as well as his obvious talent, had taken him far. He had been their epicentre when they all lived together all those years ago, their creator and destroyer she mused.

Music started up, Bob Dylan singing *Forever Young,* and to her surprise she felt her eyes fill. She was transported back to the kitchen of the house they all shared back in the day, that was where they had the record player, piles of album sleeves littering the floor in the corner by the rickety old standard lamp which Paul had found on a skip. Here was the 60's evoked, their heyday, another world, the past surely was another country. Sarah wondered how Jane was feeling, she had often thought that what happened back then had determined the course of Jane's life and hers too.

After the service people gathered in a rather nice hotel in a large, thickly carpeted function room. There was a finger buffet laid out on a long table covered with a white damask cloth. Another table had wine, beer, soft drinks. Claire had orchestrated a good send off Jane thought. She looked around for Sarah, her gaze took in the lilies on the long buffet table set out under the windows which overlooked a large garden. Soft classical music formed a background to a hubbub of chat. She overheard snippets of talk, of hip replacements, arthritis, whether to retire or not

I've never been so busy" boasted those who had

"Couldn't imagine what I'd do with myself," growled those still doggedly working or energetically in harness. Talk of insomnia, ginseng, high blood pressure, people with cancer, people who'd upped and left wives of 30 years. Pictures of grandchildren were shown, always the women who did this. It was all unutterably depressing she thought as she absent mindedly helped herself at the buffet, exchanging non committal pleasantries with people she barely knew. Some, who she vaguely remembered from university, looked curiously the same, as if they were made up to look old. She thought about Gideon, rarely seen since their university days.

Once, when he'd been married to his first wife, she had met him by chance on the tube and Gideon had invited them to one of the big parties he had always liked to throw. Howard had been keen to go but she had hated it. One second, an intense look and a hand squeeze from Gideon had been all she had got out of a night where what to wear, how to behave had dominated her thoughts for weeks. That was years ago and after that she followed his career from afar, always watching his programmes and pleased for him when he won the BAFTA .

At last she spotted Sarah and crossed the room, carrying the plate of food she had collected without paying any attention.

"Darling, am I pleased to see you!" said Sarah. The two women kissed with deep affection.

"I love your hair" said Jane "you look really well"

"So do you, my love" said Sarah .

"Well I've taken up tennis, haven't played since school but I used to be good, when I was 16," laughed Jane.

" This is grim isn´t it? Fancy Gideon dying, so unexpected, someone said he was riddled with cancer but was only actually ill for a couple of weeks" said Sarah .

"Poor Claire, awful for her, such a shock " said Jane

" She's s done very well, laying this on, finding so many people from his past" said Sarah

 "Did you see Leon in the Crematorium?" asked Jane

"No! Leon! I haven't seen him for, oh, at least 40 years! Is he here, do you think?'

Looking about Jane noticed a display of photographs on two big screens, propped up at the far end of the room. A tall thin man with greying sandy hair was peering at them. She nudged Sarah

"That's him over there. Let's go and look at the photos with him shall we?"

After rather awkward greetings:

" Sarah, Jane, still together?" was Leon's, the three of them stood silently contemplating the life that was displayed before them.

There was a picture of a young teenage Gideon with, surely it was, Davy, recognisable even then by his bushy eyebrows.

"Look" said Jane " You remember, Davy and Gideon had a band together when they were at school"

Sarah laughed at the four longhaired boys ,clutching instruments, Gideon holding a guitar.

" I had forgotten he could play guitar" said Sarah

"O, he could play anything, " said Leon." but the piano was his love"

"Clever Claire, there's a picture of Rowena," said Jane.

Graciously Claire had included pictures of both Gideon's previous wives, Rowena, his first and mother of his 3 children, was in evidence today, accompanying her son and daughters, there were pictures of her, young with her young family. Gideon had left her mired in young children all under eight, went off with his researcher, Naomi, who became wife number two. She was not here today, Jane had never met her so she peered curiously at the one small photograph of her She thought they had been married for six years or so but obviously few photographs survived for Claire's display.Then she caught her breath, beneath the picture of Naomi was a black and white picture of a group of young people, obviously on a demo, all with outrageously long hair, the girls wearing white headbands, hippy clothes and set faces. The memory of that day came flooding back, there was Gideon in the centre flanked by them all, The Ranters, Davy, Sarah , Leon, Marina ,Paul and her . Howard was on the very edge of the picture, half obscured by a banner. This seemed fitting, reflecting how he was on the edge of their lives at that time. Jane recalled with a stab of pain that it was shortly after that anti Vietnam war demonstration that Paul had died. Sudden tears welled in her eyes as she thought of Paul's unlived life. Pull yourself together she admonished herself, and shaking her head she became aware someone else had joined them.

A large rumpled man, with wild white curls,piercing brown eyes and heavy salt and pepper eyebrows gave a wry smile, nodding at the picture

"O Davy, it's you!"She said. "Look at this, it's all of us, I think it's the Grosvenor Square demo, Leon and Sarah are holding placards, and just look at Marina's Afghan coat,"

" The living are all here then, except Marina, god knows where she is" said Davy, slightly slurring his words.

Jane looked at him narrowly, Drunk? Depressed? A Stroke? All flashed through her mind then she realised, as he took a deep draught of the pint in his hand, it was the first.

She looked over Davy's shoulder, looking for Howard, she felt awkward and wanted his moral support. Davy turned to talk to Sarah and Leon and Jane said

" I'll just find Howard" She spotted him across the room, talking to someone she did not know, leaning against the bar. She hurried over and after a brief introduction to his acquaintance she said

"Excuse us please, I just want to show Howard something" .Turning to Howard she said

"Sarah, Davy and Leon are all over there looking at photos, there's some of our Brighton days, do come and see"

Sarah and Leon were talking, Davy standing alone morosely contemplating his youthful self.

"Well, Davy old boy, How's things? you don't look too good" said Howard

A split second later Jane,who had had years of practice at smoothing Howard's bluff crassness, always well meaning and invariably insensitive,

"What are you doing these days?"

"Finishing a book, farting about, fishing, waiting for death" said Davy morosely.

"Oh yes, I heard somewhere that you'd taken early retirement from Oxford" said Jane brightly.

Of all of them Davy's career had looked set to soar. After they stopped living in each other's pockets, after the events of that last summer and Paul's death Davy had thrown himself into studying, put his huge intellectual energy into academic work, got research fellowships, a PH D and finally a senior post at an Oxford college.

He basked in his maverick left wing reputation, radicalised his students, annoyed his colleagues and inevitably got passed over, his drinking became too much, telly appearances more important than scholarship. He began to be seen as a bit of a dinosaur, his causes unfashionable, his personal life messy, his judgement slightly suspect. A blood pressure scare, an increasing laziness led him to accept the offer of early retirement.

" It's all bloody grim, and this, this funeral, wretched, old Gideon, bastard but I loved him, known him since I was eleven, 60 bloody years and now he just pops off like that," he mumbled . Sarah had now joined them and made consoling noises, Leon meanwhile had turned back to the photo display
and was looking again at the picture of them all on the demo.
"Who took this photograph? I don't remember ever seeing it"
The others turned, with relief from Davy's maudlin plaint to the picture.

"I think it was one of Marina's crowd. I remember Gideon getting angry and shouting about rubbish holiday snaps when the Vietcong were dying or something. I don't know how he had the photo, I've never seen it before either." said Sarah.

Howard wasn't interested in the past but in catching up, "So Leon, amazing to see you, we didn't know you were in touch with Gideon."

None of them had seen Leon for more than 40 years, tracking him down was a real coup for Claire.

"You went travelling for a few years, didn't you Leon, India and the hippy trail?" said Sarah .

"Well, you could say that" replied Leon, giving nothing away.

"Were you in touch with Gideon?" asked Howard

"Actually, we met up in Bosnia, about 10 years ago. I was working for the British Council in NOVE SAD and he turned up with a camera crew, making a documentary. I sorted stuff for him, contacts and so on, we got drunk together a few times. "

"O,Yes, I remember that film, it was good" said Jane exchanging a glance with Sarah, maybe old enmities had been laid to rest? Leon was here anyway paying his sardonic respects to another life.

" And what about you Jane? " asked Leon, looking at her directly for the first time. "I've read some of your poems, looked at your website" Jane looked embarrassed,

 "oh, goodness. My son did that, as a school project. He's into computers"

"All sorts of literary magazines are kept by the British council and when I saw your name on, hmm, I think it was a poem called *"wet wash day"* years back I looked you up. A sad funny poem"

What he did not say was he followed up all the references to publication on her website. When they were students Jane often shared her work with him and for a few years they had kept in touch until he became immersed in work and she in domestic life.

"And you Howard" Leon turned to him, "what are you doing?"

"This and that, business, finance, play the markets, manage this fund and that, you know". Leon looked at Howard's red face; a marked contrast to his thin yellow tinged one,

" So, a far cry from defeating capitalism then? Or perhaps the collapse of the banking system a couple of years ago was you working from within? Deep enter-ism wasn't it called?"

Sarah, who had been watching Leon carefully said

" Do you still believe in it all? The dictatorship of the Proletariat, democratic centralism, the withering away of the state?"

Leon laughed " Well as I understand it here in the UK the state has practically withered away, everything privatised"

"Oh, it was all so much simpler then, " said Sarah. nodding at the photograph.

There was a silence broken by Jane who laughed in disbelief, shaking her head she said:

" Well not for me:" she shot a look at her dear solid unimaginative Howard, Howard who had saved her from the mess.

" So, Leon, are you retired now?" asked Howard.

"More or less, I've bought a house in Suffolk, do some consultancy work, and grow vegetables"

Davy's laugh rang out, "Everyone past 55 seems to be a Consultant these days, FIFAFO Fly In, Fart about and Fuck Off"

Leon looked at him and gave a thin smile.

"Well mate, I'll tell you my life's a bloody failure"said Davy

"Not supposed to bloody drink or smoke, can't hardly get it up.whats to live for?, and now my best mucker is dead"

Jane made a small comforting sound, "O, it's not that bad, I read in the paper that research has shown that 74 is the age of optimum happiness "

" Oh for God's sake Jane, you always were a bit of a Pollyanna" Davy spluttered into the dregs of his drink.

Jane blushed, Davy had always been able to discomfort her. He used to rail at her good manners, her consideration for others."Nice bourgeois Jane" was his frequent taunt when they all lived together.

"Time to go I think" said Howard, placing his heavy hand protectively on Jane's shoulder.

The room had thinned out whilst they had been talking. He wanted to get back to the office, a big chunk of the day was gone.

Jane took a deep breath, surprising herself she said

" Maybe now Gideon's dead it is time to…"

"Talk about the past, we could perhaps.. go back" overlapped Sarah

"Jolly good"said Howard "mull over old times, we are all getting on "

Davy groaned " Oh God" he raised his eyebrows " why not? I have been thinking about those days a lot lately"

Jane looked at him sympathetically, "Yes, It's our age, there's so much I didn't understand back then when we were young",….

They all looked at Leon who had remained silent. He returned their collective gaze and said, slowly,

"Well, I have room enough at my house in Suffolk for us all"

There were murmurs of agreement, efficient Sarah got out her notebook and jotted down contact details, it was agreed that they would meet up for a weekend before too long and Sarah would organise it. It turned out Davy lived in France but came over fairly regularly for meetings and events.

" Well it looks like most people are going," said Jane as they all turned away from the notice board.

" Oh god, yes I have to catch my train" said Sarah, looking at her watch .

"We could give you a lift" said Jane ignoring Howard's shake of the head

" No no, I'll get a cab, it's the opposite way for you"

"I've got a minicab coming' said Davy

"I'm going to Holborn, so I could drop you easily"

That settled, they moved as a group to make their farewells to Claire, Gideon's widow.   Jane and Sarah embraced, promising a phone call the next day. Leon had hurried off who knew where with a wave to their little group. Davy's cab drew up and Sarah and he got in the back

" Well", said Sarah " That was all very surprising"

" Old Leon, Daddy Leon we used to call him to annoy him, he has hardly changed a bit. Always aloof from the fray" mused Davy

"Gideon really respected him you know, was a bit jealous of him to tell the truth"

"What!" exclaimed Sarah. " But he was so private , so unlike Gideon and they were always rowing about politics"

" Yeh, but he was a fantastic musician, Gideon respected that and was envious of the time he'd spent in Berlin, he thought Leon had suffered more, was more authentic than he was"

Sarah looked at Davy with surprise ,

" Suffered ? authentic? These are therapy words Davy"

Davy laughed and gave her a gentle punch, they were on the back seat together in slightly closer proximity than Sarah would have liked. Davy´s male presence as always was overwhelming.

 " Being married to Janine has made me see things differently, sometimes I think I just stumbled through my twenties, catching onto one new idea then another and never assimilating any of them" This was a different Davy, different from the rather obnoxious and opinionated Oxford don who had made frequent appearances on television in the 80s and 90s , whose life had spiralled out of control, a more reflective and considered man, somehow chastened but still ebullient.

"Ignore what I said at the wake. About there being nothing to live for"

He continued

" Janine saved me, now my life is in balance and I feel peaceful. It's different, I cannot help but regret the mad old days but the pain outweighed the pleasure in the end.'

 They continued talking about Gideon, chiefly Davy reminiscing about their school days and all too soon they had arrived at Paddington,

"Goodbye and thanks so much for the lift" said Sarah getting out of the car.

"No problem, great to see you and we will meet again"

"In Suffolk" they spoke in unison, laughing Sarah moved away and Davy waved through the window as his taxi pulled out into the traffic.

Sarah hurried down the slip road to the station but saw from the announcement board that the next train was not for half an hour. The seats on the concourse were all full so she decided to go and stand outside the station and smoke the third of her daily ration. She had so wanted a cigarette after the funeral, as she lit up she mused on how no one was smoking at the reception afterwards. She had resisted [maybe not the only one?] hating the inevitable comments " what, haven't you given up yet?" Even excessive Davy had referred to not smoking. Inhaling deeply she had a sudden image of Gideon, rolling his own, with brown liquorice papers, his nicotine stained fingers deft and quick.

Finishing her cigarette she picked up a free evening paper, had a desultory look at the magazines in the bookshop and finally heard her train announced. It had been a long day.

Jane and Howard had urged her to stay with them for the night, were clearly disappointed when she refused, obviously they wanted to mull over the funeral with her, gossip about the surprising appearance of Leon, of Davy's latent desperation. But she wanted to get home, she had stuff she had to do for the charity that she volunteered for and there was the cat to feed. She got a seat by the window and eased off her smart black shoes and opened the paper, after a few minutes she realised she was taking nothing in, so bowing to the inevitable

sat back and closed her eyes, letting her mind dwell on Leon and Davy, neither seen for many years, thinking back to when she and

Jane had first got to know Gideon and the band.

 Gideon had recruited her and Jane to become their backing singers; they made a trio with the exotic Marina, a red head with wild Burne-Jones hair. Jane was a brunette and she a blonde; the three of them with the beauty and energy of youth were sensational. Sarah smiled inwardly, what would her daughter think if she knew her serious feminist solicitor mother had, at one time, briefly, attracted a following, had performed with abandon, scantily dressed, on dirty pub stages throughout Brighton?   Paul played drums she remembered, Leon bass guitar, Davy rhythm guitar and Gideon was totally wild on the piano.

 Howard was their roadie, simply because he had a van and it was a way for him to see Jane to whom he was dumbly devoted. They all, with the exception of Jane, exploited him shamelessly.

The conductor came round, breaking into Sarah's reverie. She showed her ticket, and her senior citizens rail card, and looking out of the window saw that they were approaching Reading, way to go yet. She wondered if she should get a sandwich, it would be late by the time she was home but could not be bothered to leave her seat by the window. It had been lovely to see Jane, she was looking extraordinarily well. She had told Sarah that she had recently taken up tennis again, playing with a local club in Muswell Hill. When they first became friends in their first week at university they sometimes played together but then they joined the band, started living dangerously, got into politics and tennis seemed another world entirely, a boring bourgeois world

For the umpteenth time Sarah speculated about clever sensitive Jane's life with Howard. It had been a surprise even to her, who thought she knew Jane so well, when Jane had decided to marry Howard straight after university. He was always around of course, in their second year when everything happened, there when he was needed, to ferry the band in his old post office van, to carry banners on marches where he only half bothered to understand the issues, but if Jane was going so would he.

They came from the same home town. Howard had been at school with her brothers, known her since she was 8,"She was such a sweet little kid" he told Sarah once.. It was clear he felt protective of her and when she came to the university ,where he was a second year, he looked her up straight away and just hung around .He was studying Economics, had little in common with Jane's other friends but he was easy going and always willing to give lifts, help people move flats, lend people money. Even back then he seemed very good at managing money unlike Paul who was always hard up.. Sarah remembered a conversation they had had…was it about the time she and Jane moved into the shared house in ST. Agnes Avenue? Jane, it was obvious, was utterly in love with Gideon, had changed since the first year. She had got thin and would vacillate between hectic gaiety and silent withdrawal She wrote masses of poetry then, but the only person she showed it to, oddly, was Leon. . Sarah remembered being surprised once to see Leon with a folder of Jane's work.

  Sarah involuntarily shook her head, looking out of the window,

Didcot now; she did not want to think about that time, decided to get a sandwich after all and making apologies to the man sitting next to her, pushed out into the aisle. Coming back and settling down she determinedly got out her book, a wonderful Barbara Kingsolver. Thank god for fiction she thought before losing herself in another life.

The train pulled in at last to Bristol Temple Meads, she queued for a taxi and with relief finally let herself into her flat, greeted by a mewling cat. She did not sleep very well these days and feared tonight, with the upheaval of the day, might be a bad one. After feeding the cat she got ready for bed, read a bit more of her book and finally turned off the light and settled to sleep, wondering if they really would all meet up in Suffolk.

Two hours later she was wide-awake.

Immediately her mind went back to the past. What had she done with her life, after those painful days? It was no good; she would just have to let herself follow where her introspection led. Increasingly these days she evaluated her life, weighed like evidence her actions. She was committed to left wing politics, that she had Gideon and Leon to thank for and what she and Jane had gone through turned her academic interest in feminism into activism. She studied law after her degree, became a respected solicitor working always in legal aid, for those most neglected by the system, primarily women. The surprise arrival of a daughter, Mary, had not interrupted her career, she was a single mother and life was often difficult. She relied on Jane who willingly helped her, loving Mary as one of her own brood

She was heavily involved in the Women's Movement, she was often called on for free legal advice, to draft documents and demands. She made complicated childcare arrangements so she could work and attend meetings, go to conferences., Jane who had had 3 children in quick succession, and lived near Sarah in North London would often have Mary for her. She would rush in from a meeting, pick up Mary who would cling to Jane , often she would sleep over at Jane's house. She became a spokesperson, her halo of fair hair, short then, giving her an unthreatening appearance, her warm voice making reasonable what were, after all, perfectly reasonable demands. She missed parents evenings, sports days, first boy friends, the movement was more important surely. And then in no time Mary was grown up, married and the mother of twins. Five years before she had what can only be called an epiphany, she was tired of campaigning , being serious and missed the wild and spontaneous girl she had been. She wanted a second chance, to have another life. She had been amazed how overwhelmed with love she had been when the twins were born, maybe grand motherhood would give her that chance. The pain of motherhood compensated by the joy of grandchildren. She left her job, moved to Bristol where Mary and the babies were and where she had grown up, found a nice flat and made herself totally available to her daughter's family. She had a good pension after all, she could do part time work, and she could start afresh and make up for the lost years with Mary

Of course, she missed London at first, missed Jane and other friends but her new life, a developing relationship with Mary, the children, her work, new friends, an allotment filled her days.

Often now she found her mind wandering back to her time at university. Going to Gideon's funeral today had unsettled her and seeing Leon and Davy, both so changed and so the same had jolted her. She remembered another funeral, Paul's, all of them there except Jane and Marina. They in their outlandish black clothes, clothes they had thought appropriate but surely, she thought now, they looked all wrong, like a bunch of hippies in a band, standing out from the sombre congregation in the Welsh chapel. The soft lilting voices of his parents, welcoming these English interlopers who had bedazzled their Paul. She remembered how thoughtful Gideon had been then and careful with Paul's grieving family, she had seen a different Gideon then from the confident arrogant face he usually presented to the world. Sarah sighed deeply, things looked so different from the long view, maybe a reunion weekend in Suffolk would help them all understand the past and what they had become.

A huge yawn shook her, she padded to the toilet, then, grudgingly accepting the comfort of the cat, who had sneaked up onto her forbidden bed, she put off the light for a second time and settled into her pillows.

Chapter 2: 1967

Jane woke up surprisingly clear headed, she was vaguely aware that she had had a lot to drink the night before and looking down at herself prone on the bed she realized with a twinge of shame that she was fully dressed. She remembered helping Sarah, who was giggling and pushing her away, to her room and then just sitting for a minute on her own bed and now it was morning. Thank goodness it was Saturday she wondered if Sarah was awake yet. She looked at her watch, 10 a.m., goodness, late enough to wake her surely. Memories of the previous momentous night were flooding back and she wanted to share them. She peered out of the door and along the corridor, hoping no one was around. Thank goodness there was no one in the communal kitchen, while waiting for the kettle to boil she splashed cold water on her face. There was a mirror on a shelf by the kitchen sink and she groaned at the sight of her panda eyed face. Pushing her hair behind her ears she managed to make two mugs of tea and went and knocked on Sarah's door

A muffled groan was the response to her persistent knocking and then a

"Come In" signified Sarah was awake.

"Here, tea and aspirin," said Jane.
Sarah struggled to sit up, pushed her tangled blond curls back from her face and gulped thirstily at the tea.
"oh, god thanks Jane you're a star" she groaned but immediately

afterwards

she let out a scream

"Is it true? Are we in Gideon's band or did I dream it all?"

The girls had gone to The Boat Inn the night before, they were celebrating Sarah's 19th birthday, Gideon March was playing; he was a 2nd year, a high-profile politics student, he was variously described as an anarchist, a trouble maker, a genius, master of cool, a Londoner and a brilliant piano player. They had picked up a flier the previous week and looking for a way to celebrate Sarah's birthday they had decided to go. Gideon's crowd had a wild reputation and Sarah and Jane, now at the start of their 3rd term as first years, admitted to each other so far it had not been that exciting. Not what either of them had imagined as they sweated over their exams in their last year at school. But Gideon, he seemed to be the center of all sorts of action. They decided this gig would be a great way to celebrate.

Gideon was a brilliant pianist, he could play anything by ear, could vamp jazz, honky tonk, classical, R and B
 as he got more and more drunk and stoned he would play with his elbows, knees, feet, bounce up and down on the stool until he fell off then play the keys with his chin, those nights he was completely wild and away in some frenzied musical marathon. The previous night was comparatively mild, though still rocking and Sarah and Jane had danced and danced, the long haired blond and the longhaired brunette, both full of joy and vodka. Sarah, emboldened by the vodka, sang along to Blueberry Hill, her voice sweet and smoky.

Jane joined in, both girls had true strong voices, well trained in their school choirs.

Time was called, it had been a great night and the girls regretfully gathered up their discarded belongings, Jane was rooting around under the table looking for her bag when she became aware that Sarah was talking to someone.

" Oh yeh great , thanks" she heard her say.

She emerged and saw Sarah, pink with excitement

'That was him! Gideon March! He's invited us back to his ! he noticed us ! ooo Janey!' the words tumbled over each other.

"Quick" she said 'they have to pack up their stuff and we go with them..there's a few going'

They rushed to the loo to prepare themselves for what lay ahead. It was happening!

"Oh Jane," Sarah laughed. "I don't remember much after the pub, where did we go? How did we get home?"

"You were really pissed' said Jane

" There was a tall guy, Leon I think, tall and skinny, ginger, sells the revolutionary paper on the seafront, ..."

"Oh god yes, I kept falling over and clutching him didn't I"

"He walked us back, I think it was that cigarette Gideon gave you made you go funny"

"Oo, did I make a fool of myself?"

'Well" said Jane judiciously "you did keep singing, but that was ok because Gideon asked us to be backing singers in his new band!!!"

The usually quiet Jane shouted the last bit and Sarah screamed

"Yes, yes, Fantastic! I remember! It's happening at last Jane, we are going to be rock chicks!" Emboldened by the memory, revived by the tea and full of excitement Sarah leapt out of bed and the two girls danced around the room whooping and hugging. At last they were in on the action

Sarah and Jane had made friends on the very first day of their first term. Jane was pinning up an Athena poster of Picasso's Sylvette on the cork board which covered one side of her narrow student room when there was a knock and a girl with long blond curly hair put her head round the door
"Hi, I'm Sarah, I'm next door" she looked around, her bright blue eyes taking everything in
"Gosh you're sorted!"
Jane's desk had a pile of papers and books on it, her shelves were stacked, her narrow wardrobe door shut, there was a half empty case in front of the small chest. The utilitarian lampshade had even been changed for a globular paper one.
"Wow, " said Sarah again, "my rooms still a tip.' She looked around again,
"That's so cool" she said "I love that poster, I've brought it from home too!"
Jane laughed,
"Two Sylvettes next door to each other then. That's funny . I'm Jane, I am glad you came. I've been here for ages, and am too nervous to go out on my own, that's why my room's so neat. When

did you get here?"

"'About half an hour ago, but I'm too restless to unpack, let's go and explore a bit, have a coffee in the student's union, check it all out' So, for the first and not the last time the usually cautious Jane was swept along by Sarah's exuberance and the two girls ran down the stairs and out into the campus chatting and laughing and swapping their histories. Demure dark-haired Jane, a country girl from Shropshire and bouncy blond Sarah from Bristol. They discovered they had both been to single sex schools, were both doing English, Jane had 3 elder brothers and Sarah 2 younger sisters. Sarah's parents were teachers, Jane's father a solicitor and her mum a housewife. Both solidly middle class, both eager to spread their wings. In spite of their surface differences in no time they were fast friends. They loved the same books, Sarah liked the Rolling Stones, had even been to a live gig in Richmond, Jane was a Beatles fan but that was no barrier to their friendship, they laughed, immoderately sometimes, at the same things They were young, eager for life, Sarah the leader but Jane her willing follower. They settled into university life, went out and about, but both felt there was more waiting for them. Sarah had joined the Drama society, had been very involved in drama at school and Jane the Poetry club but as first years they were low down the pecking order. Jane was intimidated by the macho visceral sub Ted Hughes verse of the mainly male members of the poetry club and Sarah disappointed to have only had a small role in the 2nd term production of UBI Roi.

They were both still searching for their place in this new

environment and now, now they were going to be in a band, hang out with the famous Gideon March!!

They got themselves showered and dressed and went down to the sea front for a celebratory breakfast. There was a cool café, Trip Out, opposite the pier where students often congregated. The walls were lined with posters, Hendrix, Dylan, Joplin, there were a couple of battered old sofas covered in Indian bedspreads, scratched and wobbly tables, a random assortment of chairs. A far cry from the tea rooms Jane and her mum popped into on a day's shopping in Shrewsbury. The girls had a sofa to themselves and ordered a full fry up. Jane was taking a long swig of her mug of coffee when Sarah nudged her nearly causing her to spill it.
A tall Pre-Raphaelite redhead, dressed in a loose flowing dress with beads hanging down to her waist was just disappearing up the stairs at the back of the café.
" Look over there, that's Marina, part of the band" said Sarah
She had turned up late at the party, Gideon had brought her over to them where they were sitting on the floor, his arm loosely draped around her neck
"Sarah, Jane, this is Marina, she will take you through your paces. First rehearsal in 2 days, 7pm at Threshers Hall. Ok?'
Marina had looked at them both through narrowed green eyes and muttered something to Gideon and then turned away. He nodded to them both and said "so, see you on Wednesday" and moved back into the throng.

"I think she's at the art school," said Sarah, spearing her fried egg and watching with satisfaction as the yolk bled into her fried bread.

"Ah," said Jane "Someone told me last night she was half French and spends a lot of time in Paris"

"Oo er," said Sarah, pulling a rueful face and "I'm from barmy Bristol and you from sleepy Shropshire, how can we compete!"

The girls laughed and finished their breakfast, then the next big decision was what to wear for the rehearsal.

They spent the next two days, in between lectures, frantically trying to decide on their look. They agreed they should be identical, they were of similar height, both had long hair. Jane was persuaded by Sarah to use black eyeliner around her eyes and was astonished at how her soft brown eyes seemed enormous and vaguely frightening. She loved it, a new persona, shy Jane replaced by Bold Jane! Sarah egged her on and they had a heavenly time laughing and parading around their austere little rooms. In the end they decided to dress entirely in black, fishnet tights, tiny short skirts, cheap shiny vest tops which they had found in The Lanes, white lips, black eyes, pre punk post beat and gorgeous.

They were on their way, they ran and skipped through the town turning heads as they went, two giddy girls on their way to meet their destiny. It took them a while to find Threshers Hall, a dingy place on the edge of town next to a Working Mens Club. They could hear drumming as they pushed open the heavy double doors. There was a stage at one end, a drum kit set up and a slight thin

faced boy, long hair to his shoulders was hitting the drums for all he was worth. The hall was large, a dusty floor, chairs stacked up around the walls, an ancient table football in one corner. Gideon was on stage, tuning an electric guitar, he shouted behind him where someone unseen was fiddling with the sound system. Jane and Sarah exchanged looks, no one had noticed their dramatic entrance, they stood irresolute but then, the doors, which had shut behind them, burst open and a burly youth fell
 in, wild bushy black hair, heavy eyebrows, a drooping Zapata moustache and a friendly eager face.
He noticed the girls
"Hey look whose here!' he shouted.
The drumming stopped and Gideon jumped down off the stage .
'Good, you came. You look great, really cool'
Jane blushed, shaking her hair to hide her red face, a habit since school. Sarah beamed,
 "Sorry if we are late, trouble finding the place"
"Got here before me anyway" said the burly boy. "I'm Davy by the way. Him on the drums is Paul, he's welsh,"
Paul shook back his floppy blond hair and waved his drumsticks at them giving them a shy smile. A tall thin figure with a distinctive roman nose and reddish brown pony tail emerged from the back of the stage.
"And that's daddy Leon" .
Leon was older than the others, had come to university late, that and his aloofness set him apart from the rest. But he loved to play guitar

and the new band was a departure for him, not being a joiner by nature. Sarah and Jane exchanged a quick look, it was Leon who had helped them home from Gideon's party. Sarah said

" Hi everyone and thanks Leon for getting us home the other night ,we were wasted'

Leon grunted and half smiled.

"hi, yeh thanks " added Jane

"So, just waiting for Marina," said Davy looking around.

"May as well skin up then"

He started to roll a joint and the six of them sat and chatted, swapping limited and edited info about themselves,it turned out Davy and Gideon had been to school together in London, had had a band at school. And then Gideon had been playing piano in one of the music rooms at the university and had heard fantastic astonishing drumming coming from another practice room. He went to investigate and found Paul, whose twin passions were dope and drumming. That was when Gideon had the idea of forming a band. Paul really was inspired and was passionate about the band., Davy of course was up for it so then they just needed a lead guitar. Quite how Leon, who had played guitar since early teens, heard about them was unclear but he turned up one day at Gideon's and was quickly recruited. They were called The Ranters, a nod to the fact both Davy and Gideon loved a good argument.

"We started off calling ourselves The Epicureans" said Gideon, shaking his long hair out of his eyes, "but we changed it, too posh, decided to change our style, get you girls on board. We want to make some money"

"Yeh to feed our habits' ' laughed Davy taking a long toke on the spliff. Sarah had tried it earlier and had a coughing fit but Paul kindly showed her how to inhale. Jane had nervously shaken her head and hoped they would still accept her in their charmed circle. All this emerged as they sat chatting but then Gideon said

'We may as well start, only got the hall for 3 hours, you girls can work with Marina once she turns up"

'Yeh I've got an essay to finish later ' added Paul

They were on their second attempt at The House of the Rising Sun when the door at the back of the hall opened a crack and Marina insinuated her way in " Like Keats' Lamia': Jane said later to Sarah when they were curled up on her bed drinking cocoa and mulling over the evening

There was something snake like about her slender form swathed in a long green crushed velvet dress with a lacy half see through bodice, her wild red hair, the colour of autumn, tumbling on her shoulders and tiny lace up purple boots.

'So 'she said 'what's happening?' Sarah and Jane soon learnt Marina never apologised or made any explanation for her appearances and disappearances, just wandered in and effortlessly drew all eyes to her.

"Hi Marina, great you made it, here's Sarah and Jane your singers" said Gideon. Marina looked at the girls for the first time, whilst they had been riveted on her since her entrance,

'O are we in costume?' she drawled looking from one to the other with a slight sneer on her face. Bitch bitch inwardly seethed Sarah and Jane, discomfited and looked at the floor.

However in spite of being irredeemably cool Marina was a good teacher and soon the girls were working out moves to the music, Jane and Sarah collapsed into giggles, encouraged by Davy and to some extent Paul but Marina was a stern task mistress. The three hours flew by and at the end they were all quite pleased with themselves leaving the hall to go for a drink at the seedy pub nearby. Marina disappeared as mysteriously as she had arrived, Davy glanced at Gideon as she left who shrugged and carried on arguing with Leon about the right chords for Jumping Jack Flash

The rest of the term went buy in a whirl, they rehearsed twice a week, Gideon insisted they should perfect a few numbers before they played in public, the end of term and the academic year was only a few weeks away so they planned a couple of gigs in out of the way pubs and then to really launch themselves at the start of the next academic year.

"The second year is a doddle " Davy reassured the girls, 'lots of time for music and fun" They were getting to know and like all the band. Davy was the hedonist in chief of the group, he it was who kept them all supplied with dope. He was a North Londoner, jewish, his politically active parents had fled from their native South Africa when things became too dangerous for them.. They were communists and his father, who was a lawyer, joined a famous left wing practice. His mother was graphic designer and Davy, as their youngest son, was given a lot of lee way . He had started smoking dope in the 6th form at school, in Brighton he would pop up to town every month or so coming back on the train with carrier bags of stuff which he would sell around the university. He was often nipping off to meet people to do deals, always had cash for drinks, was generous and generally knew just how much to smoke to keep himself happily high but not off his head. It was welsh Paul who filled the girls in on the members of the band. He was a keen consumer of Davy's deals and it was obvious he idolised Gideon. .

Once they got back to Hall after rehearsals Sarah and Jane usually sat up discussing the boys and the elusive Marina . Neither of them had met people from the London political class before, found Gideon and Davy rather intimidating in their casual sophistication.

"You know Sarah " said Jane.."Gideon and Davy are always mentioning places and bands I've never heard of, I thought Shrewsbury was a big city until I met them! makes me feel stupid"
"Don't worry, just listen and say yeh,cool ," laughed Sarah.
 She had been making regular trips to London since the 6th form, staying with an older cousin so she knew some of the places Gideon and Davy talked about and was more able to hold her end up.
    "Paul's lovely though" said Jane " he is so, I don't know.." \
"Innocent?" said Sarah.
 They both agreed Paul was a total sweetie, soft spoken, thoughtful , prone to fits of near silent laughter. He told them that he'd often been ill with asthma as a boy, spending a lot of time in bed and

oddly that was when he had got into drumming and into reading his early ill health shaping his present life.

" Leon's different isn't he? " said Jane, 'he is quiet but doesn't miss anything ,you know?'

" Hmm, there is something sort of steely about him, he is very focused ,have you noticed he doesn't smoke much blow, not like the others" said Sarah

"God, Davy! He is incorrigible" they both laughed, Davy would talk and talk when he was stoned.

Leon did not tend to spend as long in the pub post rehearsals as the rest of them disappearing off to political meetings about which he said little. He seemed to be somewhat wary of the group but gelled perfectly when they played , he and Gideon had an intense musical dialogue going .

After their third rehearsal and all the palaver and expense of loading the drum kit and PA into a taxi to and from the Threshers Gideon said

"We need to get a van, we need a roadie., Anyone know anyone with a van? "

"What about Howard?' Sarah said to Jane "bet he'd be up for it"

"Who is Howard'? asked Gideon

"Oh, he's someone from home, well friend of my brothers' really, I've known him all my life"

Jane was aware she was burbling on but was embarrassed, would Howard fit in? What would the others think of him, a bluff rugby playing 2nd year Economics student? Howard was her follower, he'd

always had a soft spot for his mate Gareth's little sister and when it emerged she was coming to Sussex he attempted to take her under his wing. He introduced Sarah and Jane to his circle of similarly conventional rather hearty chaps, all doing economics or geography After a few of these dull nights in the pub Jane said to Sarah
"o God, I don't want to hang out with someone from home"
'Thank goodness' said Sarah, 'ghastly boring crew!" So after that Jane made excuses when he suggested meeting up though she still saw him for a coffee from time to time and he knew that she and Sarah had now joined a band. He had even been nagging to come to rehearsal.
"He's got an old post office van, he's in the climbing club and uses it for that but I think he'd jump at the chance to hang around Jane" said Sarah.
" Shut up Sarah," said Jane.
"Well sounds perfect, a devoted roadie, ask him!" said Davy
Howard was easily persuaded to be their roadie, it meant he would see more of Jane and even he was impressed by Gideon's reputation and in awe of the weird beauty of Marina. Gideon put himself out to charm him at the beginning and then once his commitment was secured more or less ignored him. Davy and Paul introduced him to the delights of dope and he quickly became a bit of a bore on the comparative merits of Red Leb and Moroccan and a big fan of The Ranters.

Gideon had booked them a couple of gigs at The Boat, before the end of term, just word of mouth but Gideon's reputation was enough to ensure a good crowd to their first one

The band arrived an hour before to set up, Paul and Davy both had several joints and Gideon and Leon had pints from the bar. Sarah persuaded Jane to have a vodka and orange, to lubricate their throats. They were both agonisingly nervous, squashed into the tiny Ladies putting on heavy eye black and fiddling with their hair and stretching their tiny skirts. They were wearing high black boots, Marina had insisted, so, being the end of term and all grant spent they had to borrow some money from Davy to buy them .

"Legitimate expense" said Leon who acted as unofficial treasurer for the band, "When we make some dosh we'll pay you back" said Jane.

They emerged from the Ladies, the pub was filling up, there was an excited buzz in the air. They saw Marina standing at the side of the stage, her usual cool inscrutable self, wreathed in the blue smoke of the french cigarettes she smoked ,looking fantastic as always. Gideon, who was tuning up, motioned them to join her and then, before they knew it, their first gig had begun.

The Band played for 40 minutes, Stones, Beatles, Dylan, they were cutting edge, Gideon and Davy bought all the latest new releases, assiduously read NME and International Times, they knew what was cool, loved the music and put together a brilliant eclectic night. The three girls moved as one, Marina's strict rehearsals totally paid off; they were sexy and wild.

 O what bliss to be alive and to be young was very heaven, thought

Jane . Just before the break Gideon introduced the band by name, when he came to Jane and Sarah there was a roaring bellow from the back, Howard and some of his mates. The girls were dripping with sweat , good old Howard had got them long cold drinks and said half admiring half shocked, "Bloody hell Jane, didn't know you had it in you"

"Nor did I " laughed Jane, for the first time in her life she felt loose, free ,full of energy. The noise was deafening and congratulations bawled from every corner and then they played their second set, this one had a couple of tunes that Gideon and Davy had written,ending on a mighty version of Jumping Jack Flash. The Ranters was on its way and so were Sarah and Jane

                            It was Leon who found the house, not long after the first gig

They were all sitting in the pub, another gig before the end of term and then the end of the year. They were all worrying to a greater or lesser extent as to where they were going to live, Sarah and Jane had to move out of Halls, Davy and Gideon's Landlord had refused to renew their lease, too many complaints about noise from the others in their house, the group that Leon shared with were all third years and leaving town so all five of them needed a place.

 Paul, who lived with his mum's widowed sister in the town to save money, listened to their discussion half enviously. Since joining the band he was feeling more constrained by staying with family, although his auntie Vi

. was easy going and liked a laugh and Paul was fond of her so it seemed a good cheap solution but listening to the others as they talked made him feel envious, feel as if he had limited freedom

"Actually" said Leon "I've heard of a big house to rent, behind the station, the guys are leaving and there are 2 flats going"

"What" said Sarah " is it ok? Have you seen it"
" Would be cool if we are all together" said Davy: "is it big enough?"
"What's the drawback"drawled Gideon, pushing his tangled hair back and looking up from the cigarette he was rolling
"Cynic" said Leon "but yes there is some old girl in the top floor flat, rent controlled so that's why it's cheap maybe? But the guys say she's cool'
" ok so can we arrange to see it?" said Jane

Leon organised the key and a couple of days later they were standing outside 3 St Agnes Avenue. It was a huge house with an overgrown front garden with mature trees ,double bayed, 3 storeys high, a peeling front door which opened into a big hall with 4 doors going off it and a grand staircase going up the centre.
:'Wow,' said Davy, speaking for them all. They separated to look around, the boys going upstairs and Sarah and Jane inspecting the ground floor.
"Oh, Jane , we could have these 2 rooms on the ground floor, they're

lovely and big and there is a little bathroom in between" said Sarah excitedly /

" The kitchen is a bit dire," said Jane.

" Oh don't be so bourgeois" said Davy who had reappeared from exploring upstairs and had overheard,

" It's a great size and just needs a lick of paint and some TLC"

The kitchen was to become the heart of the household. It was big with a large battered wooden table in the centre, an assortment of wooden chairs, a rickety dresser with a jumble of dubious pots and pans and crockery and an enormous terrifying looking gas geyser over a stained double sink.

" Gosh" said Jane who had never seen anything like it, "hope I never have to light that!'

" So, I could have the big front double room upstairs , plenty of room for Marina too" said Gideon casually as they convened in the kitchen having gone over the house. Jane and Sarah exchanged glances. Marina was not with them, the Art School had already broken up and she was in Paris visiting her father. Gideon had dropped this little nugget at their last rehearsal, explaining Jane and Sarah would be doing the backing for the gig on their own.

" So," said Sarah boldly, " will she be sharing the rent too?"

Gideon gave her a look " No, she's still keeping her room at Dan's .She'll just be crashing here. I'll pay a few quid more if you like since it's the biggest room" he said coolly.

There was a slight awkward silence then they carried on working out who should have which room. Leon had been up to the top floor, there was a smartly painted door up there with a neat notice pinned to it which said Miss Pink. Next to it, under the eaves was a big attic room which Davy, once he had run up to see it, bagged and Leon took the other first floor room; he and Gideon also had a bathroom between their two rooms.

Paul, who was with them and who had been wistfully wandering into all the rooms whilst they were discussing logistics came into the kitchen and said " There's a sort of long cloak room cupboard thing under the stairs, maybe I could crash there sometimes?'

They all went to look

" Yeh, you could fit a mattress in there ,you could be our lodger!' laughed Sarah /

So it was all settled.

Later, back in Sarah's room in Hall Jane got out a notebook and started working out how much they would need for their share of the deposit and for rent and living expenses.

"Were there metres for gas and electric?" she asked Sarah .

" Yes I think so"

"Well that's easy then we can have a kitty for them and the rent I suppose we divide by five."

" Hmm" said Sarah " I wonder how much Marina will be there?"

Marina had a room over the Trip Out Café, where they had seen her the morning after the party which started their involvement with the band. Dan, the café owner and Jose, his Spanish painter boyfriend, were her flatmates . Jane had been there once when she and Howard had gone to pick her up, Marina had answered the side door and then run back upstairs to fetch something. They had hung around in the hallway , a high wall ran up the stairs covered with an enormous unfinished mural of Rupert the Bear, bright yellow checked trousers were meticulously finished, the rest still just sketched in.

"Wow" Howard had said indicating the wall as Marina came downstairs, she patted a painted trouser leg

" I fill in the squares at night when I can't sleep " she said in a rare moment of self- disclosure

"Gideon said she was keeping her place" said Jane

"Well I hope she's not around much"

said Sarah, 'She's so self-centred and unfriendly. We've been singing together all term and I still feel I don't know her "

" Maybe she's a bit shy and tries to disguise it by being superior" suggested Jane thoughtfully

"Oh Jane you are so sweet, she's not shy, she's arrogant and thinks were all beneath her"

"Well I certainly have never met anyone like her before," said Jane. "Don't suppose you would have in Shropshire! She's not just urban, she's international!"

They had gathered, from snippets from Davy and Paul, that Marina's parents were divorced, her father lived in Paris and had a young family and her mother lived in California with her third husband. She very occasionally made references to the shit progressive boarding schools she had been expelled from, no doubt about it to the girls, with their conventional backgrounds, she was exotica personified .

The girls laughed together, Marina and her world -weary air of cool disdain was so different from their bright eagerness for life.

" Well, we'll just have to see how it works out. I'm really looking forward to next year and living there with the boys" said Sarah

Chapter 3: St Agnes Avenue

The new academic year, new term and new life in the house began in September 1968. The girls had brought kitchen stuff from home. Paul and Davy raided the skips that had started to appear in Brighton, where dilapidated houses were being done up and converted into flats for the burgeoning student population. A couple of big old armchairs for the kitchen and a wobbly standard lamp with a huge brocade shade. Tables and chairs, planks of wood for bookshelves balanced on bricks also found at building sites ,for their rooms .Posters of their heroes, Che Guevara in the hall, Hendrix and Dylan in the kitchen , front covers of the International Times randomly blu tacked to walls. It was cosy and chaotic .

Marina came and went, she kept some clothes and art materials in Gideon's room but her presence was unpredictable. Sometimes she came around in the early evening and ate with them and then left, other times she would stay a couple of nights. Gideon seemed totally cool with her comings and goings.

Miss Pink, fortunately for the student household, turned out to be somewhat deaf. They rarely saw her, although to them she had seemed ancient. She had a job, left the house at 8.30 and came home at 5.30 and seemed not to be around at weekends. If she saw any of them on the stairs she would say Good evening and give them an absent-minded smile. Davy, who was next door to her in the attic had even been into her flat, had helped her fix her television one evening. He it was who discovered she worked for the council and went to stay with her elderly mother most weekends.

Sometimes they would cook and eat communally. Davy turned out to be a messy but adventurous cook, the girls both had the staples they had learnt at home, spag bol, shepherds pie, chips. Gideon rarely did much in the kitchen and Marina never, Leon was very tidy and domestic, cooked an interesting curry and was fastidious about the washing up but Paul, who spent as much time as he could in the house, earned his keep by doing most of it. He took a pride in keeping the kitchen tidy, fussed at the others for leaving mugs on the floor and not putting plates in the sink . Davy said he was worse than his mum but Paul just quietly carried on . Sarah and Jane would both have bursts of cleaning so domestically they rubbed along very well. The kitchen was the heart of the household, the communal room and centre for the late night dope fuelled sessions. Paul was mainly responsible, with Davy, for keeping the music playing, they had 2 big speakers, painted purple, that Davy had rigged up in the kitchen, the occasion, more than once, of fuses blowing .

Their taste was eclectic, some tracks got played over and over again, there was always music. They had all gone to see Jimi Hendrix at the Dome, it had been Jane's first big gig and she had been blown away, mostly by the immense energy of the Brighton crowd. In the kitchen they played Hendrix, Procul Harem, The Stones, The Beatles, The Grateful Dead.,The Who. Gideon and Davy were always buying new albums, read the NME assiduously. Astral Weeks by Van Morrison was a huge favourite of both the girls, Paul of course was an avid fan of Cream and Ginger Baker the crazy red headed drummer and Leon especially loved Bob Dylan. For Davy it was Eric Clapton…

One evening Davy burst into the kitchen where they were all assembled, including Marina, surprisingly draped over Paul's chair, with him perched on the sagging arm.

" Listen to this guys, it's so cool" he said, taking Dylan from the turntable and turning up the volume , Dont Bogart that Joint by Fraternity of Man blasted out.

Don't bogart that joint my friend,
Pass it over to me,
Roll another on
just like the other one"

Laughing Davy skinned up another one

"I've got some great Leb" he said and they all settled in for a night of it. Sarah made tea, Gideon got some cans out of the rusty fridge.

"Why Bogart" asked Jane, after one puff, passing the joint onto Leon

"its Humphrey Bogart, you know the movie star" said Leon, inhaling in his turn

"yeh, Maltese Falcon, great movie" added Gideon.

"he always had a cigarette burning during long speeches and never took a drag" explained Leon

"So man, don't bogart that joint" sang Paul.

Each time the chorus came round they all joined in. Sarah collapsed into helpless giggles, passing the joint on to Leon she said, coughing

"phew this is good stuff"

Marina ,who had not joined in the singing, stretched, and in the process knocked Paul off the arm of the chair. He lay on the frayed Persian carpet, another skip find, kicking his legs in the air. This provoked even more laughter from Sarah and Jane joined in

"oo Paul you ok?" she said gasping with giggles

"Yeh, its great down here" he said, resting his head on Gideons foot which happened to be next to him.

"This is getting silly "said Marina. "why don't we play a game, get to know each other better?"

She looked challengingly at Gideon, he knew her games, but he nodded,

"yeh.. .o.k. cool"

"So I am thinking of someone in this room, you ask me questions, like if this person was a colour what colour would they be and you all try and guess who it is. Whoever guesses has the next go"

" oh I've played this before," said Sarah.

Marina looked at her "Yeh right, so, ask me a question then"

"If they were an animal what would they be?"

"cat"

"IF they were a car what would they be?" asked Leon

"rusty banger"

"what drug?" asked Davy

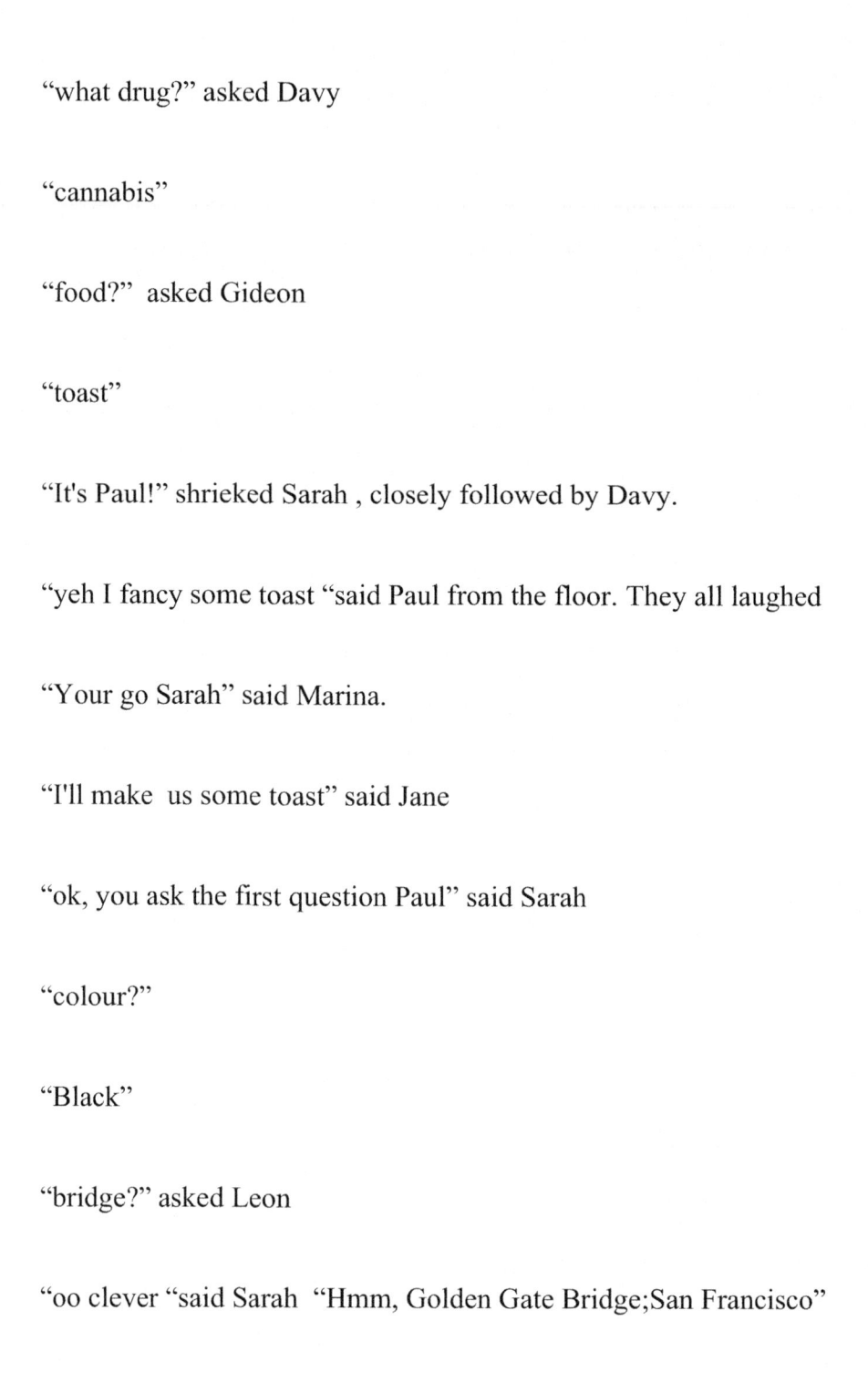

"cannabis"

"food?" asked Gideon

"toast"

"It's Paul!" shrieked Sarah , closely followed by Davy.

"yeh I fancy some toast "said Paul from the floor. They all laughed

"Your go Sarah" said Marina.

"I'll make us some toast" said Jane

"ok, you ask the first question Paul" said Sarah

"colour?"

"Black"

"bridge?" asked Leon

"oo clever "said Sarah "Hmm, Golden Gate Bridge;San Francisco"

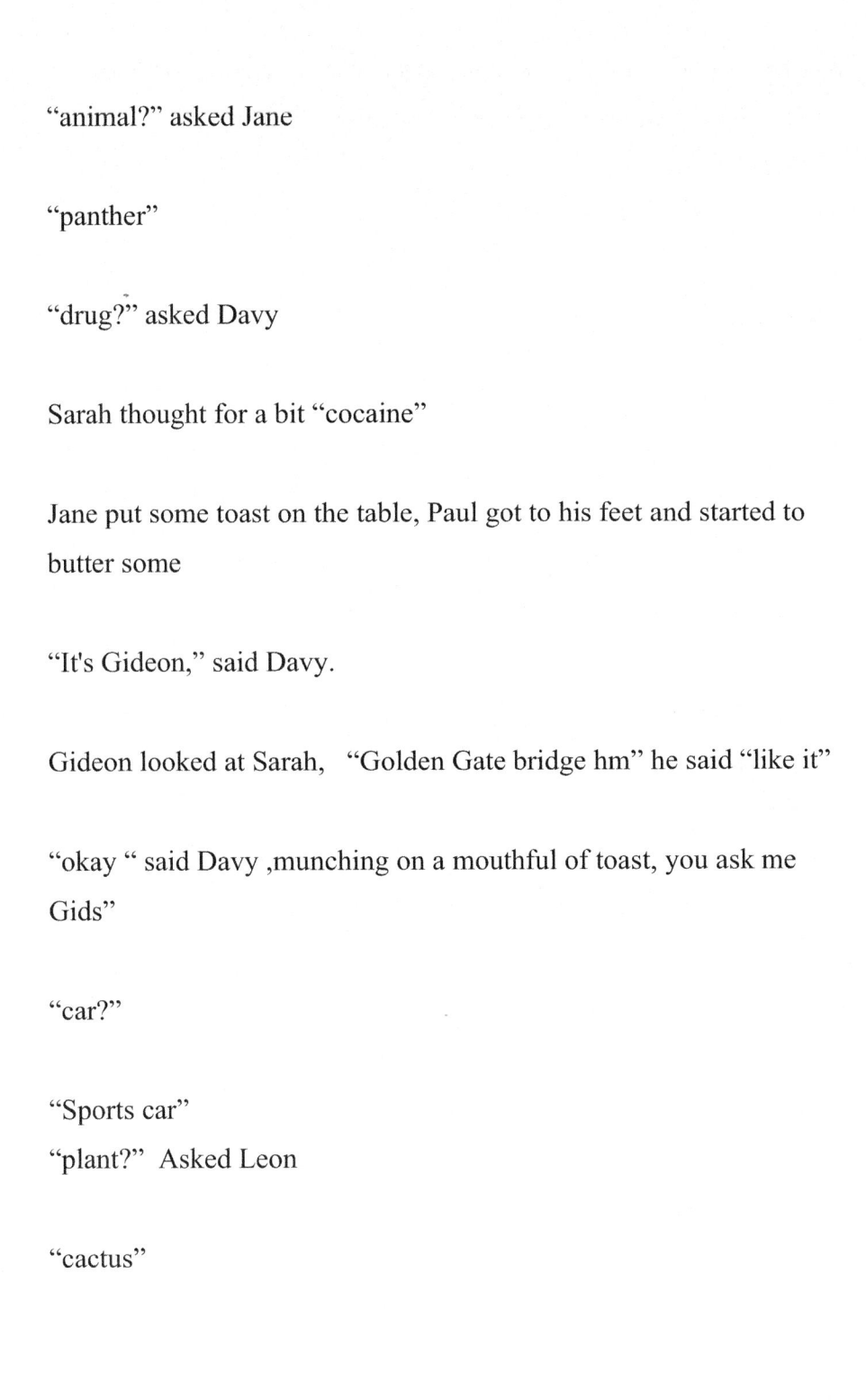

"animal?" asked Jane

"panther"

"drug?" asked Davy

Sarah thought for a bit "cocaine"

Jane put some toast on the table, Paul got to his feet and started to butter some

"It's Gideon," said Davy.

Gideon looked at Sarah, "Golden Gate bridge hm" he said "like it"

"okay " said Davy ,munching on a mouthful of toast, you ask me Gids"

"car?"

"Sports car"

"plant?" Asked Leon

"cactus"

Sarah and Jane exchanged a look, it was obvious already who this was but they both wanted to hear more of Davys answers

"drug?" asked Gideon

laughing Day said "heroin"

"animal?" asked Paul

"Fox "

" How banal" said Marina "I suppose it's me"

They continued to play, Marina answered questions for Jane, pink, morris minor, mouse, cocoa, aspirin...cruel and discomforting. Gideon guessed and answered for Sarah, yellow, mini, chipmunk, red wine, cannabis, Clifton Suspension Bridge and Paul did Davy . Red, Ferrari, monkey, hamburger speed. They were all helpless with laughter, the music played, Paul fell asleep on the floor, Davy kept starting the same story over and over and then forgetting what he'd said, Leon nodded sagely and occasionally spoke words understood only by him. Sarah leant on Davy, Marina enigmatically gazed at Jane who put her head down on the table. More toast was made, Paul woke up and made some custard…..the night wore on in stoned disarray.

Next morning when a bedraggled Jane went into the kitchen only

Leon was there, tidying up.

" Wow, that was some dope," said Jane.

"hmm, I think you and I smoked the least last night, guess the others wont appear til much later"

Jane stretched and yawned:

"Actually I don't feel too bad...do you think I`, m a mouse and aspirin ?" she asked Leon, half laughing. .

" Oh Jane, Marina is a bitch,anyone different from her and she lashes out . She does not like your calm."

Jane blushed, "My calm?" she asked.

"Yes well, you seem so self sufficient ,your quietness carries a charge you know"

Jane busied herself making some instant coffee and thought about what Leon had said. That was not how she felt inside but liked the impression Leon had of her .

"Do you fancy going to one of my favourite places today?" asked Leon suddenly

Jane looked at him surprised, they had not spent any time together just the two of them

"Oh maybe, where?"

"Brighton Pavilion, have you been there?"

"oh no, have been meaning to, would really like that . I'll just get dressed..ready in 10 minutes."

Leon looked after her as she left the kitchen, it was on an impulse that he'd asked but felt pleased with himself that he had.
They left the sleeping house and headed towards the sea front. Jane was wearing an old fur coat she had acquired in the Lanes and Leon the long army greatcoat he always wore.

"So, why is the Pavillion your favourite place?" Asked Jane

Leon did not reply immediately, Jane waited, already marvelling at the towers and cupolas as they approached the iconic building.

"Well" he began hesitantly "The first time I saw it I could not believe my eyes, I come from a Northern industrial town" he paused ,

"hmm, Sheffield, yes" said Jane

"I don't know if you have been to the North but our public buildings are all about power, wealth, solidity and common sense. Big, square, Georgian style reeking of hard work and pride and the Pavillion is the exact opposite, it is pure fantasy, frivolous and hedonistic, a pleasure dome."

"Kubla Khan" said Jane

"Exactly. Wait until you see inside, its mind blowing"

They paid their student reduced entrance fee and entered the exotic dream of another man and another time. The mughal inspired interiors ,the sumptuous embroidered hangings, the fantastically painted ceilings took Jane's breath away. She had never seen anything like it. They wandered through the vast rooms, Jane occasionally stopping to admire intricate mirror work, the embroideries. As they wandered Leon told her how the Prince of Wales built this as a holiday home where he could entertain his mistress and indulge in excess away from his disapproving mother .It was he who had made Brighton fashionable and gave it its rakish reputation. When they got to the music room Jane said :

"But this is all Chinese not Indian at all"

"oh Prinny was eclectic in his tastes , anything exotic ornate and eastern appealed to him"

Jane pondered on the strangeness of people. Leon ,so austere and controlled, enamoured of this rich and excessive place . Leon watched her wide eyed responses ,he was glad he had suggested this outing, glad she seemed to get the place.
"O Leon, it's a marvel it really is , but somehow silly…"
He laughed " Exactly ! It's so unbritish , out of control…".

After an hour or so they left and with unspoken agreement sat down on one of the benches in the garden. A companionable silence passed and then Jane said
 " Would you mind if I asked you a personal question ? "
"It depends what it is ,but no go ahead"
" So how come you came to Uni later than us ?" she asked.
 Her brow was slightly creased, she was hoping she had not intruded into his guarded privacy.
" Well, my last year at school my mother was ill, I didn't think Icould leave her"
" oh I'm sorry"
No she´s ok now but it took a while, Depression. So I got a job in a factory, she got better ,could work again ,I went to Berlin ,then applied and here I am" several difficult years summarised in 2 sentences .
"That's why you're different isn´t it" said Jane… "lived much more than us,even Gideon. "

Leon laughed "You could say that. Come on, let's go down to The Tune In and see if the others have surfaced"

They found Sarah and Davy, nursing their heads . Apparently Marina and Gideon had not surfaced yet and Paul had crawled back to his aunties for more sleep. Jane was pleased with her outing and planned to go back to the Pavillion again on her own, she quite understood Leon's fascination with the place and felt she now had something of a grasp on her most enigmatic of housemates, barring Marina ofcourse.

Another aspect of life at St Agnes Avenue were the political arguments that often blew up. Everything was changing, the Vietnam war, the civil rights movements, the student activism in Germany, left groups proliferated , new clubs, galleries, coffee bars were opening all the time. Davy brought OZ into the house, the subversive outrageous magazine Australian Richard Neville had started in 1967 , they read the International Times, far far removed from the Times. Leon was always picking up left papers, Class Struggle , Black Dwarf, pamphlets produced to mark the sit-ins at London School of Economics.

Gideon and Leon in particular would have fierce arguments, Leon because he really cared and Gideon out of an innate contrarianism. He had grown up in a political household, his father had been elected a Labour MP, in 1966 when Labour had won the General Election with a huge majority, his mother was a journalist and he had been around politicians and journalists all his life. The Gay Hussar in Soho was where all family celebrations took place. He had a brother 10 years older but by the time he came along, an afterthought, his parents were fully immersed in their careers so he had had a lot more freedom than many of his peers,. his parents were fond but busy and benignly neglectful . At 16 he was hanging out in John Dunbar's Indica gallery and The Roundhouse, had been to hear Ginsberg and Corso at the Albert hall in 1965 and was experimenting with dope. He and Davy were wild boys, Friday Saturday and Sunday they lived a life on the edge of the pounding heart of the alternative revolution that was going on in London and during the week, both very bright, they kept it together at school with Davy doing a bit of dealing in the 6th form and both of them trying to sleep with as many girls as they could. Gideon was ferociously ambitious, music was his current passion and a good way to pull but he was interested in all the arts, loved films and on dates would take girlfriends to the Hampstead Everyman. Gideon's politics veered between the libertarian left, he had experimented with LSd on his 18th birthday, Timothy Leary"s mantra of turn on tune in and drop out was infinitely appealing, as were the radical politics of Marxist Leninist groups that were proliferating amongst the student left.

 Davy. With his communist South African background contributed a wider world view to the kitchen arguments, he had briefly joined a Trotskyist group at school ,more to annoy his father than deep conviction. He was a magpie, picking up and discarding theories in a way that infuriated Leon and exasperated Gideon. His consumption of mind altering substances made focusing on any particular line for long. problematic

. Leon's background could not have been more different from his housemates. He and Paul were the resident proletariat, teased Davy, both from the working class and should be in the vanguard. Leon was from Sheffield , he had been born in 1943,the result of his father's only war time leave. Shortly afterwards his father had been sent to Burma and was captured, spending the rest of the war in a Japanese prisoner of war camp. He returned a broken man , in poor health and subject to appalling nightmares. He died when Leon was 6. Like Paul Leon was an only child and the first in his extended family to go to University ,if belatedly. He had got involved in class politics when working in a factory after he left school. This was the time of developing far left politics in Sheffield rent strikes, apprentice strikes, Leon found an outlet for his intellectual energy in Marxist politics and activism. In the summer when he was 21 he met Hans, a German socialist student from the free university of Berlin over in Leeds to visit. relatives . Leon was drifting, was becoming frustrated with the monotony of factory work and having a bit of money saved jumped at the chance to go back to Berlin with Hans. The 6 months he spent in Berlin ,attending the occasional lecture but endlessly talking with the radical student groups that were beginning to flex their muscles convinced Leon he should go back to studying,

So, two years later he was here in Brighton, studying politics and arguing with his housemates.

Gideon and Leon's arguments reflected their different positions, both loved the cut and thrust of debate. Gideon would get more and more forceful, sharp witticisms at Leon's expense, frequent insults and obscenities. Gideon embraced the Trotskyist idea of continuous revolution, Leon believed in democratic socialism and the leadership of the working class. .Gideon called him a Stalinist, mocked his logic and Leon would get icier and icier and more precisely articulate. Davy would join in ,he loved to argue too but would often go off on a stoned riff, causing Gideon and Leon to exchange looks ,eager to get back to their own dispute. Davy was swayed by what he read ,the people he met,was an avid reader of Red Dwarf and the International Times and would get hung up on some obscure thinker . At first their rows discomfited the others but soon it just became part of their lives, enjoyed by the principals and tolerated by the others. The name of the band was a nod to the English civil War, a period both Gideon and Davy were interested in , though Gideon inevitably supported the Ranters and Leon the Levellers .

Sometimes, when the arguments got particularly heated Paul would interject. The first time he did so, when they had not long lived together, had the effect, for once, of silencing Gideon .

Paul was lolling in his usual old armchair, legs over the arms and drawing deeply on his joint when he suddenly he said

" I know communists, lots of important early ones came from my village in the Rhonda from the 1930s we been known as Little

Moscow. People went to fight in the Spanish civil war from our place , it's in our blood this stuff youre talking about. We live it"
This was the first time Paul had revealed anything much about himself, his usual comment was "cool" or " right on" something had inspired him to make a claim over these middle class boys, a claim of authenticity that he had not known he had . He was overawed by the others, Gideon he hero worshipped both as a musician and as an amazing person, in Paul's eyes just about everything he did or said was cool. And Davy, his confidence, his wildness ,his roaring laugh sometimes overwhelmed him.

Paul had won a scholarship to a very good school in the valleys and the school encouraged him to apply to university. His dad was a miner in Maerdy, his mum a cleaner. He was an only child and his passion for drumming, his brains and his introversion, he was a very quiet boy, puzzled his parents. When he wanted to go to University and to study philosophy in spite of having scant idea of what that meant they encouraged him to apply to Brighton, where his mum's widowed sister could keep an eye on him, make sure he ate properly and be around for him. However, mostly Paul slept in the cupboard under the stairs, just going back to his aunties a couple of nights a week ,usually with his washing.

Sarah was the first to speak after Paul's intervention, asking him more about the history of Maerdy and of the miners' struggles over the years.

For Sarah these evenings of talk were an education, she was becoming interested in politics as the student movements in the US and Europe gained momentum. She had been active in CND at school, had been on the later Aldermarston marches , and was keenly interested in the world. Sometimes she saw an old school friend when she went up to London who was at LSE, a centre of turmoil . There were American students there , bringing ideas of the personal is political, later to be fully embraced by feminism. Until now she had not joined anything, keeping an open mind and trying to make sense of all the conflicting ideas and movements that seemed to spring up monthly . She listened eagerly, asked questions, read some of the names Gideon would quote to support whatever line he was maintaining. Later Sarah came to realise Gideon had only skimmed Gramsci, Marcuse, Marx and all his other heroes. He was a magpie, could construct a towering edifice of argument on scraps of hard fact. It was this which would drive Leon to distraction, he was scholarly, thoughtful, had recently joined a Maoist discussion group at which Gideon sneered.

 As for Jane, coming from an unthinkingly Tory family, apart from supporting CND and trying to understand what was going on in the world through careful reading of the Sunday Newspapers, she had not previously thought much about politics. She was never sure whether the insults which flew around, Trotskyite, Stalinist,running dog, bourgeois scum, arsehole, were meant . She had been brought up to believe that politics was mens´ business and should never be talked about at the dinner table[one of her mothers maxims] and would eventually retire to her room to get on with some work, uneasy with the invective.

As for Marina , when things hotted up she would yawn and say " God boring, I'm off" and either leave the house altogether or disappear upstairs to run a hot bath, naturally using up all the water .

Chapter 4 : Swinging Sixties

They had been living together about a month when, one morning, Jane knocked on Sarah's door,

" Do you want a cup of tea Sarah"

"Make it two" a male voice replied, followed by the sound of scuffling and laughter.

Jane retired to the kitchen to put the kettle on and a few minutes later a tousled haired Sarah appeared tying her old towelling bathrobe. Jane raised an eyebrow and Sarah pulled a funny face

'it's only Davy" she said " Davy?"said Jane

"oh, you know, we were the last up last night, talking, he came into my room for a last joint and, well, you know how it happens."

Jane did not know how it happens, she was still a virgin, sometimes she thought she must be the only virgin left in their year, in the town, in the whole of swinging Britain. Everyone seemed to be doing it, the songs they sang in the band were all about sex, the papers and magazines, all about sex. Davy sometimes bought Playboy, for the serious interviews he said, and Jane glanced at articles about sexual practices she had never imagined, pictures of naked bunny girls, sexual problems that were beyond her comprehension

That evening the girls were curled up on Sarah's bed, Bob Dylan was playing and they were having a restful cup of tea together.

" So said Jane ' are you like together now, you and Davy?"

" Oh Sweetie no, we're just good mates really, we don't have an exclusive thing going, I'm not possessive, that's not cool, no-one should like, own anyone else. You should be free. To sleep with who you fancy, you know"

" But don't you feel jealous or anything?" Jane asked hesitantly.

'Well, look at Marina" said Sarah. "She does just what she wants and with who she wants and Gideon doesn't mind. Nobody owns anyone else's bodies,"

Ever since moving into St. Agnes Avenue, Sarah had become aware that Jane had been developing a passion for Gideon. She often talked about him and when he spoke she listened with rapt attention. She also knew Jane was frightened of Marina and would not dare do anything about it.

At the mention of Gideon Jane blushed, she hated to think of Marina, her snaky limbs coiled around Gideon. She said what was uppermost in her mind:

" And what about love?"

Sarah laughed "What about love? Oh I don't know. I'm not in love with Davy, he's a laugh, it's nice having sex with him"

Jane blushed again. Sarah had lost her virginity at 16 had had a steady boyfriend and after that ended slept with a couple of other boys before coming to university all of which she had told her friend.

" We have really good discussions, he's interesting and in the band and it's sort of easy really. He helps me with my essays for Social Science which is worth it too!"

The conversation then moved on to speculations about Marina.

They girls often talked about her, Jane with an appalled fascination and Sarah with an early feminist anger:

" well, the thing is Marina can wind any man around her little finger and she does it by being hot and cold, she is so manipulative, she always seems to get what she wants"

Sarah was smarting , earlier she had been in the kitchen to search for biscuits for them to have with their tea, Marina was there and had ignored her, barely looking up from the book she was reading. Then Paul came in and Marina was all smiles, took her feet off the chair so Paul could sit down

" She's such a cow, she is only interested in men, thinks women are invisible and beneath contempt. Well I think she is contemptible" Sarah had a faint inkling that cheerful Davy the arch hedonist was himself, in some way, a bit in thrall to Marina, nothing she could put her finger on but that sense added to her annoyance

" But she is so beautiful, " said Jane." Girls like that they expect to get their own way with men"   She found Marina thoroughly intimidating. Early on in living in the house Jane had wandered into the kitchen one morning to make a cup of tea, she was wrapped in the Marks and Spencers dressing gown that she had had since the sixth form. Marina was sitting smoking at the table, drinking coffee. She had a stained Japanese silk kimono open over her naked body, her breasts exposed, she glanced up at Jane, grunted and carried on drawing in her sketchbook. Jane felt about 5 years old and scurried back to her room brooding on Marina's lazy sensuous grace.

There was something deeply elusive about Marina , she never had cosy chats

with them, no swapping of clothes, getting ready to go out together ,giggling and laughing. . Once a sequined red mini skirt vanished from Sarah's room. A few days later she saw Marina wearing it.

" Is that mine ?" she asked her. Marina gave her a long cool stare "No of course not"

   Sarah reported this exchange to Jane "She is an absolute bare faced liar. How could she?" They looked at each other in amazement

"Gosh" said Jane., Marina's cool effrontery took their breath away.

The sequined skirt had come from one of Sarah and Janes expeditions to The Lanes. Sarah and Jane had taken to haunting the junk and vintage shops in the Lanes, the rundown quarter of narrow alleyways and squares near the sea front. They had acquired an impressive collection of net skirts, boas, army jackets, sequinned bodices, droopy chiffon dresses, natty waistcoats, slippery satin robes. Each time they came home with a haul they would have a dressing up session, shrieks of laughter, twirling and swirling around Jane's room. Paul took to joining them on their forays and also after some persuasion in dressing up .

"Come on Paul, try this on," said Sarah late one Saturday afternoon after a successful trip. They had come in, smoked a joint and were giggly and happy.

She held up an oversized fringed tie dyed shirt in pinks and blues. Jane was sporting a huge army coat, looking in the full length mirror, the reason why they always had these sessions in her room.

"My dad would be so offended if he saw me in this".

"Yeh, especially since you've only got a bra and pants on underneath" laughed Sarah

Meanwhile, Paul, who had been rummaging in the pile of clothes on the bed, held up a pair of pink satin trousers

"How about these?" he said "be cool with this shirt?"

"Fantastic" the girls said in unison

He pulled off his jeans and wriggled into them then stared at himself in the mirror. He turned around and looked at his back, did an unconscious wiggle and then to the girls shrieks started to fashion parade around the room

" Oh Paul, you look fab " said Jane

"You are sooo cool," said Sarah.

They had never seen Paul so uninhibited, the clothes had unleashed something hidden in him, he pranced and paraded for the laughing girls.

"I know lets do your make up" said Sarah.

Yes, Jagger wears eyeliner, lots of musicians do" added Jane

"well okay but let's skin up first" said Paul.

While he was doing that Jane made a notice FASHION SHOW AT 6PM and went and put it on the kitchen table.

"Well all get dressed up and made up and then go and surprise the others". she said.

"The band can have a more theatrical look, more on the edge, androgynous, like Bowie or Jagger sure Gideon would be up for it"

Looking up from rolling a joint Paul said

"Not sure Leon would wear a dress" they all laughed.

Sarah carefully smoothed blue eye shadow onto Paul's eyelids, Jane passed her an eyeliner pencil and she drew a thin line on his upper and lower lids.

"you're good at this " said Paul

"yes my kid sisters were always mucking about with my make up and I used to do them"

The three of them had a great time putting on heavy makeup, Paul, with his floppy blonde hair was transformed, Jane had become a siren and Sarah a film star. Egging each other on they chose the most outrageous outfits of their haul, Paul had completely fallen for the satin trousers but swapped the tie dye for a flowery old lady blouse . Sarah had a flouncy satin robe over a lacey vest and tiny orange skirt and Jane put on the tie dye with a huge buckled belt around her slender waist and bunched her hair up into a top knot. . Finally they draped strings of beads around their necks, a pound would buy half a dozen in the junk shops,They tied scarves around their hair, put on red red lipstick and were ready.

There was a knock at the door..Davy called out
\
" what's happening? We are all in the kitchen waiting for the show"

Sarah opened the door a crack
"Put The Kinks on ,for our fashion show"

The music blasted out and first Sarah, then Jane and finally Paul entered and sashayed around the kitchen ,the others whooped and cat called, Davy wolf whistled at the girls and Gideon whistled at Paul, Leon watched smiling sardonically

"So what do you think? Our new style" said Sarah " sexy, ambiguous, timeless, hippy, crazy"

"No way you'll get me dressing up" said Leon

"o we know that grandpa " mocked Sarah

"yeh ,no problem you looking straight adds another level , is it ironic? Subversive? I like it " said Gideon .

" Next gig we'll fancy up, Marina might be pissed off , not to have been consulted but think she'll go for it. "

As it happened Marina, though insisting the 3 girls should look more or less the same embraced the new image, now before gigs they vied with each other to look more and more outrageous, all the boys wore makeup, even Leon allowed Sarah to do a toned down version of eye make up. Davy with his moustache and stocky muscularity always looked male but Gideon was wonderfully languidly ambiguous and Paul utterly embraced the feminine even wearing his eye makeup to lectures.

St. Agnes Avenue seethed with sex. Gideon and Marina led a semi-public affaire, though both of them seemed to sleep with other people. When Marina was not in residence, which was quite frequently, sometimes different girls would stumble, with tumbled hair and swollen lips, into the kitchen in the morning to make Gideon tea. Davy and Sarah slept together quite often and sometimes each of them would have someone else. Leon would occasionally bring a serious intense comrade back with him. They would sit up discussing Marxism Leninism until late and then spend the morning in bed. There was one girl, Rachel, who stayed over quite often for a couple of months but then vanished. Neither Sarah nor Jane liked to ask what became of her; Leon was reticent about his life both past and present.

"For all we know he could have murdered her for having the wrong political line" said Sarah

O no, don't be silly," said Jane but the thought haunted her for a while.

Paul and Jane were the only celibates in the household and Paul mainly because he was too stoned most of the time and because his emotional energy was fixed on Gideon. The only thing that really got him going was playing the drums, then he and Gideon were often as one, which seemed to be enough.

Ever since the first night at the pub, when Gideon had casually asked them both back to his place, Jane had been fascinated by him. She had never met anyone like him, his energy, his confidence in his body ,his rudeness, his style. He was so different from the previous rather serious and conventional boyfriends she had had. Howard, although never a boyfriend, was a classic of the type, tennis club, rugby, hearty but good mannered, irredeemably middle class. Gideon was rough and rude, had a vociferous opinion on everything., the intensity of his physical presence sometimes overwhelmed her . Oh and how he could play the piano. His surprisingly slender hands flew across the keyboard or caressed it with sensuous delight. It was his piano playing that she fell in love with first then his confidence, his verbal fluency and dark good looks. She watched him covertly whenever they were all together. Gideon did not take much notice of her; she was too reticent for him. However once or twice, when they were performing, Sarah caught him looking at Jane speculatively She had a true voice and could really move,

" Dampened fires there mate" Sarah had overheard him say to Paul .

After rehearsal one night Sarah said to Jane:

" I know you fancy Gideon" she continued to speak over Jane's blushing protests

"Look it's obvious, he just wants a good time, believe me he's trouble, totally untrustworthy."

Not for the first time Jane said, "Well anyway Marina and he are a sort of couple, I know that"

" Yes," said Sarah slowly. As she had explained to Jane before she and Davy were not a sort of a couple, funny the way Marina and Gideon were in spite of their frequent diversions with other people.

" But he does what he wants and I know you, you would get too involved, you would get hurt and it would all be a big mess."

"Don't worry, he never even notices me," said Jane sadly.

It was a Monday evening in November that it happened.

She was alone in the flat, Marina was away somewhere , Sarah had accompanied Davy on one of his frequent trips to London, Leon was involved in a sit-in at the Art college and had been gone for days. Paul was at his aunt's and she sat in her dressing gown in the kitchen reading Andrew Marvell and sipping cocoa. Gideon's voice rang out

"Anyone in? And he burst in to the kitchen, threw his bag on the floor and reached in the fridge for a can of beer

" Oh, hi Jane, anyone here? " he asked, as if she was no one.

"Only me" Jane's heart hurt, her mouth was dry. He seemed in a bad mood, slumped down into one of the battered armchairs and morosely swigged back a can

"Alright?" she said nervously

"No I'm not fucking alright. Spencer gave me a lousy mark for my essay, Bloody Marina's fucked off who knows where, I've got a sodding great overdraft and its fucking raining."

" Oh dear " said Jane with a small smile "sounds bad! "

Gideon looked at her for the first time since he had come into the kitchen; her dark hair newly washed spread out on the shoulders of her soft blue dressing gown. She looked a picture of calm serenity, in fact Jane's smile was a nervous rictus, her calm the frozen state of a rabbit in the headlights of his attention.

"What are you drinking?" he asked.

"Cocoa"

"Oh sweet little Janey, all clean and ready for bed and having your bedtime drink" He wasn't sneering, his words sounded strangely wistful.

"You're lovely "he said "So uncomplicated, not like that bitch Marina" he moved to sit beside her, " She's fucked off to Paris, things are kicking off and she always likes to be where the action is, doesn't give a shit about the band or art school" then he sounded off about his essay and all the time Jane made gentle comforting noises, scared to spoil this extraordinary mood of intimacy. After a bit Gideon gave a huge yawn

"Let's go and lie on your bed , have a smoke and keep talking, " he said.

In a daze Jane lay beside him, he stroked her hair, she felt both blissful and tense, enjoying the feel of his body beside her.

"Lovely little Janey " he murmured, a hand slipping inside her dressing gown and tweaking her nipple. A stab of desire went straight to her groin, she could hardly breathe for excitement. Then they were kissing and Jane was lost.

Later Gideon said " That was nice, was I your first?" when Jane blushingly mumbled yes he kissed her more and said she was delicious. Then he fell asleep.

Next morning Jane woke up to the amazed realisation that Gideon was in her bed, arm flung over the side, what she had longed for had happened.

She remembered everything, the soft words he had whispered in her hair, his strong and energetic love making. She felt sore and sticky, normal she supposed and crept out of bed so as not to disturb him and went into the bathroom. Clean, shining, bright eyed she left a cup of tea beside the still sleeping Gideon and flew off to class. The day passed in a dream, as she listened to a boring lecture her mind went over and over the events of the previous night. At the end of the day, on the way back to the flat, she passed the flower seller outside the station and on an impulse of joy bought a big bunch of mixed chrysanthemums.

"Where did these come from?" asked Sarah, coming into the kitchen, straight from the London train. Davy was hard on her heels

"Hi Jane, you look full of beans," he said.

" Oh, I bought them," said Jane. "How was your weekend, you were gone a long time?" Sarah and Davy settled down to talk about the event they had gone to at The Roundhouse, the people they had hung out with, Sarah showed off the second-hand purple boots she had bought at Camden Market, Laughing, talking over each other Davy and Sarah had clearly had a great time. Paul wandered in

"Hey man, I've brought some great stuff in town " said Davy and started to roll a big joint. Next came Leon who started to tell them how the sit-in was going. The kitchen was full of talk and laughter, smoke spiralled in the air, Paul made toast, and Jane hoped and hoped for Gideon's return. Finally, just when she was thinking she should go and get on with some work Gideon breezed in with a carrier of cans.

"Hey man," he said first to Leon "How's it going?" He passed round the beer, looked at Jane for the first time and said "Hey Janey" and Jane's blush crept up her neck and suffused her face. Sarah threw her a sharp look, and then looked at Gideon. The evening turned into a bit of a party. Davy went out for fish and chips for them all.

Later, worn out by nervous excitement, Jane was the first to get up and say she was off to bed. The strain of being in the room with everyone when all she wanted was to kiss and kiss Gideon had got to her, Gideon had paid no more attention to her than normal, in fact had paid most attention to Leon with whom he had been arguing about direct action. "Night " said Sarah "We'll catch up tomorrow"

To a chorus of grunts and goodnights Jane left the kitchen. Much much later when she was lying half asleep her bedroom door opened and it was Gideon. He slid into bed beside her, she curled towards him and into his arms, he was naked and whispered " "Hello my lovely little Janey"

Two weeks passed, days went by in a blur for Jane, she went to classes, chatted to her friends, even wrote an essay but she lived for the secret private nights of gentle intimacy with Gideon. He was quite different when they were alone in her room, as well as making love he would talk about his family, his relationship with Marina

"You give me such peace Janey" was one of the things he had said which she rolled around like a precious pearl in her mind. He did not come every night, probably four or five times over the next month but enough times for the others to realise what was going on.

" Everything alright Jane?" asked Sarah, noting Jane's shiny hair and sparkling eyes

"Oh yes, please don't worry, I'm happy, it's ok really" she would not be drawn into any confidences but hugged this new delight to herself.

"Well, be careful," said Sarah and Jane smiled,

And then Marina came back. Jane had bought food on the way home, she and Sarah were going to make a Spag Bol for everyone, she had also bought some cheap red wine, her step was light in spite of the weight of the bags and her heart sang, maybe Gideon would come to her tonight? It had been several nights since they had slept together and she was missing him deep in her body.

There were voices in the kitchen when she got in. Marina was leaning back in a chair, her long mini skirted legs, ending in short red suede boots up on another chair. She was talking to Leon and Paul, turned her head to look at the new arrival, seeing it was Jane she tossed her tangled red hair and said "O, Hi" and carried on telling Leon about Les Eventements. She was excited, for Marina, positively animated, she had been marching with French students, hanging out at The Sorbonne, staying up all night drinking endless espressos …her eyes glittered and her face was pointed and white.

Sarah was washing up, wordlessly she raised her eyebrows at Jane and then the 2 girls busied themselves, chopping onions frying the mince. Jane's heart clenched in her chest as she chopped and stirred. She listened to Marina but most of all she listened for Gideon's step. Davy breezed in then, finally, Gideon. A pause fell on the bustle and Marina looked up through her long lashes at Gideon, "Salut " she said. Jane stared hard into the pan of mince she was stirring, every little drop of fat was crystal clear, time stopped, there was a thundering noise in her ears. Nothing happened, Gideon lent down to kiss Marina, opened a beer, Davy rolled another joint, Paul stretched across his chair, Leon sat straight quizzing Marina about the slogans and demands of the French students. The long evening wore on, the food was eaten, wine was drunk, joints were smoked, talk and talk, Marina febrile and high, Gideon loud and witty, Jane silent. Of course Jane was often silent, however both Sarah and Leon glanced at her from time to time but she seemed composed, seemed interested in all that was being discussed. Eventually Marina stood up, stretched her long slender body, her tight orange tee shirt, a bold clash with her red hair, clung tightly to her beautiful breasts

"I'm knackered " she said "Coming Gideon?" and she went to the door, Gideon, without a glance to anyone, got to his feet and followed. A momentary silence fell and then they all began talking at once, except Jane, who sat, stricken. Then she too got up and silently left the room.

"La Belle Dame Sans Merci has returned, " said Leon.

"Oh dear" said Sarah

After an interval she went and knocked on Jane's door, pushing it open she saw Jane's form bundled under the blankets and muffled sobs emerging from the depths.

"Oh darling, what did you think would happen when she came back?" she asked, stroking what she could see to stroke.

"I don't know" wailed Jane

Marina had a vague sense that Gideon, who she considered belonged to her, was drawn to Jane in some odd way. Sometimes she would look at her with narrowed eyes. She would be casually possessive of Gideon who, occasionally would throw Jane a rueful smile . On such tiny indications Jane would build hopes and fantasies

That winter it was very cold and they all spent most of their time in the kitchen. With the oven on, door open and a gas cylinder heater on full blast a lovely fug built up quite quickly. None of them worked in their rooms, the uni library was warm so the flat was for sleeping and socialising in the kitchen. Marina was around more than she had been but mostly stayed in her and Gideon's room where she plugged in a double electric fire which meant the meter was always running out.

"No big deal" she said after Sarah complained

"I'll pay" and she ostentatiously left bags of change next to the meter. Somehow Marina always seemed to have plenty of money . She was constructing a huge collage on the floor in the bay window. Things would vanish from the kitchen, the potato peeler, a chopping knife , a grubby tea towel, all incorporated into the collage. Once Sarah and Jane crept up to the room to look, screaming faces torn from Leon's Solidarity with Vietnam newsletter, the missing kitchen knife, reams of tissues torn into red flowers, earth and stones, all meticulously arranged in a grid, it was a violent disturbing piece. Marina was a mystery that was sure, and to Jane a terrifying one. Jane told herself sternly that she must stop obsessing about Gideon, it was just casual like Sarah said, and had only happened because Marina was away. At night though her memories of their love making haunted her, no matter how hard she tried to bury herself in work, in having fun with Sarah, Gideon was always at the back of her mind.

Chapter 5 : 1968

They all went home for a couple of weeks at Christmas . In the new year Paul brought a runty kitten to the house. His aunt's cat had littered and this one was the last to go. Jane, who loved cats, took the mewling sad little scrap to her heart. Marina hated it, and it always seemed to crap in Gideon's room in spite of Jane and Sarah's artfully placed cat trays. Marina would kick them " Fucking filthy cat" she would say and it would hide from her, frequently under their bed which just made her angrier. Jane, who was often first in, would check what the kitten had been up to but one evening Marina trod in a pile of cat shit as she went upstairs and shouted,

" That bloody cat, I'm off I'm not staying here until its house trained" and slammed out the front door.

Gideon came to Jane that night, the first time for weeks. Jane had almost given up hope, had tried to convince herself it had just been a brief fling for Gideon .

 Lying in his arms after they had made love she tried to talk to him about how she felt, knowing as she falteringly said she'd missed him that Gideon was irritated . He moved away from her and lit a cigarette.

"Come on Janey," he said, "you know the score. No possessiveness right? Be cool little lady"

" Yes, sorry , it's just lovely to be with you " she said

Feeling stupid and conventional she attempted to bury her feelings, to go with the flow, accept that Gideon needed his freedom, she tried so very hard to be cool.

Sometimes she would drink too much, then she felt ok, that she was free and going with the spirit of the times. The household knew what was going on but Sarah was the only one she talked to.

However her late night talks with Sarah became more constrained, Sarah wary on Jane's behalf of Gideon's selfishness,

" He is a taker Jane, don't let yourself get too involved, keep it casual"

"I know, I know" Jane would sigh " but I'd rather have a bit of him than nothing"

She dwelt on each time he came to her bed, hugged to herself his words, built castles of hope from scraps. One night he said to her, after having a blazing row with Marina which the whole house heard "Janey your'e my good angel, sometimes I think Mariana is the devil"

When she repeated this to Sarah in an unguarded moment Sarah's frustration with the situation exploded

" o Jane, it's the old dichotomy, Madonna and Whore. You are the Madonna, that's not really you, it's what he wants you to be . Like all men he wants his cake and too eat it. Honestly!He really makes me sick!"

After that Jane was much more circumspect, withdrawing from Sarah and becoming instead increasingly close to Paul. One night, when the band had a gig and Marina was particularly flamboyant and wild, drawing admiring looks from every male in the pub and everyone was going on to a party she went disconsolately home alone, saying she was tired . She crept into bed and brooded about the hopelessness of competing with Marina. Much later her door opened and Paul came in. Paul's cupboard was next door to her room, divided by a thin partition, this was not the first time he had heard her restless in the night

:Hey Jane, what's up?" he asked ,coming over and sitting on the bed. Jane sat up, pushing her tangled hair off her face, the kitten was curled up beside her , it was obvious she had been crying,and with her woebegone face there was something both tragic and comic about her.

" oh Paul,

"It's Gideon, It's all so awful, I want to be with him all the time but Marina has a hold on him and she looks at me as if I'm some pathetic nurse or something who she allows to have a few nights with her man. I hate it, I hate her, I'm so miserable. I only feel alive when he is with me. Sarah thinks Im pathetic, Davy is embarrassed by me, Leon too and stupid Howard is always saying everything ok Jane when of course it is obvious it is not.. oh shit"

After this long speech Jane dropped her head in her hands and sobbed. Paul put his arms around her and patted her back, murmuring words of comfort. The frustration and tensions of playing a role,of trying to be what Gideon wanted had finally become too much.

Paul, who also worshipped Gideon, eternally grateful to him for the band and his chance to play the drums, was a good listener. He rolled a joint for them and lay down beside Jane.

"You know Jane, Gideon is not like other people. I think he is a genius, he is so …one woman would not be enough for him, you are so lucky' he said this wistfully," to have what you have with him.He chose you and needs you"

"Do you thinks so?" sniffed Jane

"Yes yes I do, Marina is a witch, she has some sort of hold over him…he needs you to balance her"

He was wary of Marina, she made him feel uncomfortable, she seemed somehow aware of the feelings that he had for Gideon, feelings he could not even acknowledge to himself.

To him it was an honour to be taken to bed by Gideon, his defence that he was not like other people soothed Jane.

"You're not a one night stand Jane , he says you're an angel, you give him peace he needs you even if it does not seem like it."

Paul was very fond of Jane, the two quiet listeners in a noisy household, they were drawn together. He would offer her crumbs, assure her that she was special to Gideon, that he had seen him looking at her, such crumbs sustained Jane and brought her and Paul ever closer. This was the first of many late night sessions the two of them had. She felt she could no longer talk to Sarah about her feelings, They were still close , talked about work, the band, the others in the house but Gideon was now off limits

Paul soothed her, enabled her to get through the days and nights when Gideon was elsewhere.

One night, they were all together in the kitchen , except for Marina who was out of town again. Jane had cooked a big bean stew and Gideon was sitting with his arm loosely round her. Paul was smiling at her through clouds of smoke, Leon looking tight round the mouth, why was that thought Sarah? Davy doing his irritating thing of jiggling his leg to The Doors who were blasting out on the record player. Jane got up

"Good night everyone" she said

 "Yeh' said Gideon, getting up too and following her.

Leon and Paul went off to their rooms which left Sarah and Davy alone .

"Honestly!' exploded Sarah " He is just using her! As soon as Marina is back he ignores her . I hate the way he treats her, hot one moment cold the next "

" Cool it Sar" said Davy. "It's not our business, she's a big girl "

"O for God's sake! What is it with you men? Sticking together? She's not like me, she's vulnerable, surely you can see that? And that Marina..she is a man eater, a cow!'

Davy looked discomfited as he had reason to do .

   Sarah wasn't the only girl Davy slept with at St. Agnes Avenue. One night he was lying in bed in his attic room, reading, about 2a.m. when the door opened. It was Marina, flame hair down her back wearing a man's slippery paisley dressing gown, quite evidently naked underneath. He looked up in surprise

"I can't sleep," she said. " Give me a cigarette"

Davy leant over to the orange box that served as his bedside table and passed her the packet and some matches. She sat on the end of his bed. His thickly curled hairy chest was the focus of her amber eyes

"I see you are an Esau," she breathed through a cloud of smoke

"What?"

" You know, Jacob was a smooth man and Esau a hairy one. In the bible, idiot. Gideon is a Jacob"

Davy found it hard to make sense of her, his eyes mesmerised by the perfect globe of her left breast, which tantalisingly revealed itself as she inhaled on the cigarette

"What do you know about the bible?" he scoffed.

"Oh one of my shit schools was a convent, if you had detention you had to learn bits of the bible, I spent a lot of time in detention until they expelled me" said Marina. She never spoke about her childhood, her home or from whence she sprang so this was a revelation almost equal to the perfect breast.

She leant across him and stubbed out her cigarette. He could hardly breathe.

" Well" she said, smiling a predatory and deeply sexual smile,

" We might as well" and she slid off the dressing gown and slipped in beside him in one slithering movement.

When Davy woke up the next morning she was gone. He stretched and felt a sting of pain across his back. He craned around to look in his small mirror and saw livid red scratches down his back. He shuddered with remembered pleasure, that was some fuck he thought. He felt rather awkward when he went down to the kitchen but Marina was nowhere. She did not come back to the house for a couple of days, the next time he saw her was when they played a gig at the Bull. She merely nodded like she usually did and when he made a small move towards her she froze him with a long cold stare from her amber eyes.

And that was how it was, once in a while she would appear in his room, just often enough to keep him slightly on edge. . Once, when they were all together in the kitchen, including Gideon, she gave Davy an imperceptible nod and said

"I'm off . See you " and left the room. Later when he went up to his attic she was there.

"What about Gideon?" he said

"What about Gideon? " she replied.

"Well you know"

" No I don't. Don't be boring " and she reached out of the bed and unzipped his jeans.

Sarah knew there was no way Davy would criticise Gideon, Paul shared Jane's adoration of Gideon and Leon, he kept firmly out of it though clearly felt sad for Jane's misery

Jane clung to the emotional roller coaster she was riding , working, rehearsing the band, waiting for crumbs from Gideon
One day the kitten disappeared. Sarah was home first, usually the Scrap came rushing to greet everyone and mewed her tiny mew, Sarah called and looked about downstairs but no sign. As the others came in they joined the hunt. All sorts of stuff was found under beds but no kitten. Gideon and Marina came in together. He looked at Jane's woebegone face and went up to his room ,crawled under his bed , moved heaps of clothes and had a good search but she was not there. It got late.
"For god's sake" said Marina . " Its only a bloody nuisance of a cat...probably fucked off where there's better pickings" she narrowed her eyes and watched Jane as she spoke. Jane went white, looked wildly round, obviously choking back tears and left the kitchen
Next night Gideon came to her room.
" Sorry about the cat Janey and Marina. She can be a bit heavy sometimes " he said . "I guess Scrap must have got out, I went up to ask Miss Pink and she hasn't seen her"
Jane's eyes filled and he put his arms around her and kissed her. She clung to him tightly and pressed her hot face into his shoulder
" Its ok" he said and stroked her hair .
"Where's Marina?" she asked into his chest
" She's gone back to Dan's for a bit"he said
The next few nights Gideon slept with Jane and so it was, whenever Marina was away Gideon would turn to his gentle peaceful Janey.

She learnt not to tell him the truth of how she felt, to be grateful for the times they had together. Her moods would swing wildly, she took to smoking, partly because of spending so much time with gentle stoned Paul.

Howard, Jane's devoted follower, was conscious that Jane was different, often on edge or oddly excited . He did not know what to make of her ,one night when they were loading the van after a gig he said to Davy

:   "Is Jane alright? She seems different."

Davy laughed,

"Yeah, well, she's getting it and doesn't know how to handle it"

Howard went bright red. Jane? His school friend's sweet innocent kid sister?

"What do you mean? Who?" he asked.

Davy nodded his head at Gideon who was coming out the pub door, Jane beside him both laughing, Jane was happy, the gig had gone well, Marina had not turned up, maybe it was a night for her.

Howard went even redder and finished loading and with a grunt got into the driver's seat

Chapter 6:   March 1968

They were all really busy, as well as the band and classes the anti Vietnam War campaigns were hotting up, with demonstrations across universities in America, in Berlin and Paris . Tariq Ali had called for demonstrations in London and Leon, Davy and Sarah hitched up to London to a meeting in early March and they all decided to go on the big one, March 17th ,there was to be a rally in Trafalgar Square, Tariq Ali and Vanessa Redgrave were going to be among the speakers. Leon was particularly active, giving out leaflets and organising the coaches which would go from Brighton

Davy and Sarah were both involved with an agit prop theatre group which put on happenings on the seafront, focusing on the war. Marina was spending a lot more time at the Art School, helping make posters and banners to take on the march , lending her mysterious glamour to the student collective .

On the day of the march the six of them left the house together at 8a.m ,grumbling and yawning. They had sat up late the night before, discussing the earlier demos ,the horrors of napalm, the brutality of the American government, and the demonstrations in the US. Davy had met a guy in Brighton who was an American draft dodger,he dropped a lot of acid and talked wildly of revolution going on, said Davy, who had hung out with him a few times. They talked some more about the next day's march, Leon telling them again what had happened last time and speculating what might happen this time. Gideon and Davy were both veterans of CND marches, but Jane had never been on a big demo before and was glad that Howard had decided to come. Secretly she knew he couldn't care less about the

Vietcong but hoped maybe the speakers at Trafalgar Square would change his mind. She knew she would have no chance of hanging out with Gideon and rather ashamedly she acknowledged to herself that it would be reassuring to have Howard a long. Davy had given them all his parents phone number " Just in case anything happens" he said. They knew his dad was a solicitor and had said it was cool to call him if they were in any trouble.

They got to the bus station where they met up with Howard and Marina. She was with Dan and Jose and other art students, she had a white bandage tied around her wild hair as did many of the others Sarah whispered to Jane " Trust Marina to start a trend."

Dan and Carl had an enormous banner on poles which took some manoeuvring and much joshing to get on to the coach. 10 coaches left the car park , Leon fussed at the front with a mike, he was in charge of their bus .

" We'll be parking up near Hyde Park," he announced, "when you get off make sure you check where we are, and make a note of the registration number . We'll be leaving at 7pm , if you are not coming back with us let me know before you get off. We won't' wait so be sure to get back here on time "

"Yes teacher" shouted Davy from the back and there was laughter, Leon gave him the finger and sat down, turning to talk to John, another of the Brighton organising group. The trip had the atmosphere of an anarchic school outing , one without teachers ,where you could smoke, have a joint, move around the coach,shout across the aisles. Singing and chanting broke out intermittently as the bus sped along the A23 .It was a Sunday , traffic was light and they made good time. Once in London Davy led the way on to the tube at Marble Arch , it was full of students en route to Trafalgar Square, for once Jane was glad of Howard's unflappable bulky presence beside her as they all pushed and shoved their way off the tube. The Banner, and other placards which Gideon and Davy were carrying, came in useful as they pushed their way through the crowds. As they crossed the Strand they could hear a great roaring chant HO HO HO CHI MINH , Sarah,holding onto Davy's hand ,was excited and breathless. It felt fantastic to be with so many people ,all focused on the same thing. She tied the white bandana that Marina had distributed on the coach around her blonde hair, Davy did the same ,his thick curls and lopsided grin gave him the air of a pirate rather than a revolutionary. They stood together, a group of them from the coach, by the tube exit on the edge of the square . " If we all get separated remember to be back at the buses by 7pm ' said Leon.

Jose and Dan, unfurling their banner at last, said in unison " look out for the banner". John produced a camera and took their photo. "We're not on bloody holiday," growled Gideon. "
'Fuck off 'said Jon, " I am making a record, maybe an art project or something and .." his words were lost as the crowd roared ,Tariq Ali, leader of the SVC , up on Nelson's plinth ,had passed the microphone to Vanessa Redgrave. She too wore a white bandana around her head. They all moved into the crowd, Sarah and Davy , followed by Jane ,Howard and Paul pushing forward to hear the

speeches. They got nearer into the crowd, Jane looked round for the others but could not see them, she thought she glimpsed Marina's hair, but wasn't sure.

Then the speeches were over and everyone moved off to the American Embassy, the real target of this mass gathering. Gideon and Marina had vanished but Paul glimpsed Leon with the big Brighton banner. The march headed towards Marble Arch, every now and then they all broke into a run, marshals with VSC arm bands shouted to everyone to keep up. The rumour was there were German students, and Rudi Deutschke at the front, it was they who were setting the pace. All around was noise, chanting, singing. They passed a cafe and Davy said

"quick, lets get a coffee and then we can wait for the Brighton lot" They stood, the 5 of them, drinking the horrible but hot coffee and watching the crowd, a jazz band from Leytonstone CND marched by , a group of women with pushchairs, lots and lots of hair, denim, afghan coats, headbands, placards, banners and always the chants " who did you kill today LBJ? " Ho ho ho chi minh, out, out, out , the roars, the music and the energy were phenomenal.

The girls grinned at each other, this was great , every now and then they saw someone they knew, especially Davy, and suddenly he was gone, running after a friend from school that he had spotted.

"Lets try and stick together" said Sarah to Jane , realising she was unlikely to see Davy again until they all met back at the coach. The Brighton banner came past and finishing their coffee they fell in behind it, Leon was taking a turn carrying one of the heavy poles and then they reached Grosvenor square.

A metal fence had been erected around the square to protect the embassy . The leaders of the march wanted to present a petition to the embassy, they wanted to get in . Those at the front were pushing and pushing against the fence, Howard, who was taller than the rest could just about see what was happening. There was a new shout , "The fence is down". More and more marchers pushed from behind, Howard held tightly to Jane's hand, Sarah and Paul hung onto each other. Suddenly there was

a new different noise above the roar of voices , the sound of galloping hooves as mounted police men appeared from the side roads leading into the square, horses neighing ,screams as the police leant down and flailed right and left with their batons. The four of them were swirled and pushed as they all tried to get out of the way of the horses, they were so big, Sarah and Paul were terrified, not so Jane and Howard who had grown up around horses Jane was crying " It's wrong, it's wrong, the poor horses." A wild eyed long haired student in a torn denim jacket was trying to pull a police man off his horse, others were joining in , horses were rearing, their hooves kicking out desperate to find purchase. They were pressed together , bottled up in the crowd of people and horses Paul groaned as a glancing blow from a baton hit his shoulder, Sarah was furious, angry and scared and determined to hold her ground , a police man leant from his horse and grabbed her by her coat, "Fuck off Fuck off " she screamed and struggled. Howard, big rugby playing Howard shouted above the melee,

"Hold on to each other", he wrested Sarah from the tenuous grip of the policeman, leaving him holding an empty coat and pushing and pulling, shoving with his elbows, butting people in the back got them all to safety, at the edge of the square.

Jane was crying and still worrying about the horses, Sarah was shaking with anger and fear, Paul was white and sickly ,his shoulder throbbing dreadfully, Howard was flushed but exultant. " Just like a Bloody rugby scrum " he said. Sarah had lost her coat, Paul needed aspirin, Jane could hardly stand , down the road they could see a crowd standing outside a pub. "Come on , that's what we need " said Howard. He was in his element bursting with testosterone and adrenaline. He pushed into the crowded bar, his height and loud voice meant it did not take him long to be served, the others sat outside on the pavement. Everybody was taking to everybody else, swapping rumours and experiences. When Jane said something about the poor horses a red headed girl with a grubby face said "oh no it's ok they are specially trained for riots "Everyone was drinking thirstily, bloody but unbowed, the atmosphere was a mixture of shock and excitement.

"Did you see what the pigs were doing man? They were out to fucking destroy us. American lackeys ."

Later, still together, the 4 of them got back to the coach, just before 7. They were all weary and foot sore, Paul had got some aspirin from a chemist en route but his shoulder throbbed. Sarah was mourning the loss of her coat ,a purple velvet coat from Biba, Jane was quiet, she did not know the police could behave like that, and she kept wondering what had happened to Gideon. Leon was at the door of the coach checking people off, "I saw Marina and Gideon,they said they'd hitch back tomorrow, they are going to a party somewhere ' he told them.

"All I want is a hot bath and bed " said Sarah " no way I could party" " Well, that's them isn't it " said Paul ,admiringly. There was no sign of Davy so at 7.30 Leon decided the coach should set off, it would take a while to get out of London with all the other coaches from all over the country trying to do the same thing.

"O I expect he´ll go to his folks, he'll be ok " said Sarah to Jane .

Gideon and Marina came back late afternoon the next day, bringing news that 200 people had been arrested, it turned out one of them was Davy. He appeared a few hours later driving his mum's car.

He burst into the house shouting " I'm back"

The girls emerged from their rooms, Gideon came bounding down the stairs

"Hey man ,what happened to you" they moved into the kitchen, Paul was there reading the papers that Gideon and Marina had brought back with them

" Some fantastic photos here, of the police charge," he said . Leon appeared and got some beers from the fridge.

"So Davy tells us , where have you been "

Davy's words came out in a torrent

" In the slammer ,the pigs, they pushed a whole bunch of us together and just picked us off. We lay down in the road and 4 fat ones picked me up

" Did they hurt you" interjected Paul, his shoulder still hurting badly

"Nah, just gave me a shaking really ,then we were all bundled into this van and we drove off. They dropped 2 of us off at this weird little police station in Hyde Park. I said ", he laughed "I demand my rights. I want to phone my solicitor. Did not say it was my Dad""

"What was your cell like? ' said Sarah curious

" o bare ,bucket loo in corner, hard bench bed" said Davy airily.

"my dad turned up about 2 in the morning and we went home"

"Was he angry? " asked Jane .

"well pissed off at having to get up at 2 am but no, he and my mum got arrested loads of times in South Africa, this was nothing . anyway think quite proud actually and mum has lent me her car to take my stuff back"

The Easter holidays were about to start. They had one last gig, the day before the end of term and then Davy drove Sarah to Bristol before heading for London and Howard took Jane home in his van . Gideon and Leon were staying up, Finals were looming for them. Paul rarely went home and Sarah said he could crash in her room over the holidays . Marina ofcourse went to Paris, the French students were occupying the Sorbonne, les eventements were hotting up.

"Trust Marina, "said Sarah jealously, "to have a dad who lives in Paris !"

It had been a fantastic term, agreed the girls . Jane, when she could forget about Marina and Gideon , was loving her course, losing herself in books. She was also writing a lot of poetry , her intense emotional state was soothed and calmed by the sadness and joy she worked to express in her poems.

Writing helped her understand and cope with her feelings. Once early in the new year Leon had come into the kitchen when she was working on a poem. She thought the house was empty and the kitchen was the warmest place to sit. He;d asked what she was writing and they had a long talk about poets they both liked. Although he was studying politics Leon had a deep love of poetry ,particularly the first world war poets. After that Jane would sometimes leave her folder of poems in Leon's room, so it came about, that oddly, he knew more than anyone her feelings about Gideon and the effect on her life. Sarah was increasingly involved in politics and agitprop street theatre, she and Davy had been working with other english and drama students devising and performing short plays on the seafront, warming themselves afterwards in Dan's cafe . The last night before they went home for the holidays the girls talked over the term, they had played some brilliant gigs, the band had been great ,they had had a memorable party at the house ,one weekend when Miss Pink was away , the Grosvenor Square demonstration had been a major event for them all.

" You're alright aren't you Jane?" asked Sarah as, finally, they talked about their relationships with Davy and Gideon.

" Oh yes ,of course ,all cool" said Jane, airily, keeping to herself the dawning realisation that her period was 2 weeks late.

2,400

Chapter 7 : Despair

The first few days of the Easter holidays Jane hurried to the toilet each morning hoping there might be blood in the bowl. Every tiny twinge in her stomach had her running upstairs to check her knickers. After a few days at home,where, as ever, her mother had laid on lovely meals, her brothers had teased her and her dad would say,looking lovingly at his sweet and only daughter,

"Everything alright with you dear?"

Jane began to long to be away from their loving attention, to be with Gideon and the others in the discomforts of St. Agnes Avenue and to focus on what was happening to her body.

It was spring, the daffodils were out, the chills of winter had passed and everything was green and fresh. She began to hope her period would not come, to fantasise about having Gideon's baby, they were a bit young but he was taking his finals in June, she could have a year off and then he could look after their baby whilst she went back to uni. The picture she conjured was of a happy loving little family, Gideon always said she gave him peace, was sometimes gentle and sweet to her, surely he would be excited about the baby?

Alone in her childhood bedroom Jane allowed these fantasies to grow until the real Gideon, with all his complications and selfishness had gone to be replaced by a brilliant loving father and husband.

She decided to go back to St Agnes Avenue early, she longed to tell Gideon the news. Her parents easily accepted her excuse of work to catch up on, of rent paid for the holidays so silly not to be there . They saw how happy she looked,

"Our girl has a real glow to her" said her mother the evening before she left. "must be in love," said her dad.

" Well she certainly is enjoying university, singing in a band, going on demos, falling in love is all part of it eh?" agreed her mother.

The journey could not go fast enough, finally just after 4pm the train pulled in and Jane ran from the station to the house. Would Gideon be there? He had said he wasn't going home, was going to revise for the looming exams, Leon was staying up too with only a couple of days off visiting his mother in Sheffield. Marina had gone off to Paris again, the fact that she was away had helped Jane decide to go back early,it would be like when she and Gideon had first got together Marina was in Paris then too.

Letting herself in she noticed Gideon´s battered ruc sac in the hall.

" Gideon are you there?" she called .

Gideon came running down the stairs from his room, he was wearing his leather jacket and carrying a bag. Her heart skipped a beat, he looked so handsome, his thick black hair was newly washed, he looked alert ,excited.

" Janey" Gideon wrapped his arms around her

" What are you doing back, thought you weren't back till next week"

"Oh, I wanted to see you ,to tell you something," said Jane, taking off her coat and trying to sound casual.

"Hey ,it's great to see you but I'm off to London in a minute, to catch the boat train to Paris, you've only just caught me" He led the way into the kitchen, ʹ

"I´ll put the kettle on, sit down ,guess what's happened?"

Not waiting for an answer he rushed on, he'd borrowed a film camera from someone in the Art school, he was going to make a film about the happenings in Paris, Marina had got to know some of the student leaders, had fixed up an interview for him with Danny the Red, Rudi Dutschke the German student leader was in Paris , it was all coming to ahead. He was bursting over with excitement, did not notice Jane's silence and bare acknowledgement of his plans .

Eventually he stopped talking, looked at his watch then, noticing Jane's silence said "Hey whats up? Aren't you happy for me? It's a great chance and it'll be a gas"

I´m pregnant" Jane blurted out. This was awful, not how she'd imagined telling him at all.

An eternity passed, one second passed,

"Oh what a drag for you" said Gideon. " don't worry, Marina knows someone who'll sort it . No problem , don't worry. We'll deal with it when we get back" He bent down to kiss Jane who was sitting numbly at the table.

"Must dash for the London train. See you" and he was gone.

Jane put her head on the table and howled. No baby, Marina and Gideon would sort it out. Marina would fix her up. Oh god, the humiliation, Marina laughing at her with Gideon, stupid Jane getting pregnant. The stupid dreams she´d had of Gideon and her and a baby. She was stupid, stupid, stupid. He did not care at all, what a drag for you he'd said, as if it was nothing to do with him. The injustice, the carelessness made her cheeks burn with anger and despair.

After a while she wearily got up and went into her room, she looked at her blotchy tear stained face in the mirror. Finally the reality of her situation hit her. She was in the middle of her degree, her parents were so proud of her,they would be horrified, she was only 19, she couldn't have this baby, Gideon obviously did not care at all, she must have been mad even to imagine he would want it.

What should she do? She did what she should have done as soon as she knew she was pregnant and phoned Sarah. Sarah, after a short silence said she would come back the next day

" Have something to eat, love and get some sleep . We'll manage don't worry ,I´ll help you, it will be ok I promise"

Jane cried herself to sleep, acknowledging for the first time that she meant very little to Gideon, and also for the first time seeing him for what he was, a selfish self obsessed young man whose emotions were shallow and self serving. The only one who had a hold on him was Marina, and that was surely because she did not care what he did.

Sarah took charge straight away, since the first year she had been actively involved in the Abortion campaign, had marched, distributed leaflets in support of liberal MP David Steel´s private members bill, the Abortion Act had been passed in 1967 . In fact, she reminded Jane, The Ranters had done a benefit in support of the campaign at The Fleece in the high street. She was very clued up but since the bill was not yet law they would have to wait and see what Marina could do to help.

"Don't worry darling, you won't have to talk to her or anything I'll find out who she knows and come with you and everything .It will be alright. Concentrate on thinking positively and I know a 3rd year who had an abortion somewhere in Hove last winter, I could ask her too."

The next week passed in a blur of misery for Jane, she tried to work, tried to carry on as if nothing was happening but her lank hair and dull eyes belied her repeated assurances to Leon and Davy that she was ok. When Paul came back she confided in him, Paul and Sarah were her comforters, Paul the most since he just held her and made soothing noises. She could tell Paul about her silly dreams and hopes and he understood. Since he hero worshipped Gideon he did not slag him off like Sarah but talked of his genius and how ofcourse he could not be a father yet, he had to become famous as he surely would,he was not like other people. somehow this made Jane feel better about herself, less pathetic. After all, how could she expect a giant like Gideon to be tied down with a baby just at the start of his life? Sarah on the other hand was outraged at Gideon´s cavalier behaviour.

"He is such a shit, only thinks of himself ,typical man"

It was during these difficult weeks that Sarah shifted from being a supporter of the nascent women's movement to being an activist, set on the path which would determine the rest of her life. She began to realise how women's consciousness was shaped and determined by a man's world and women could only be free if they examined everything they had believed about themselves.

 When Gideon returned from Paris he was alone but he was rarely in the flat, as well as trying to cram three years knowledge for the looming exams he was spending evenings at the art school trying to edit his film. ,Jane avoided him as much as she could without it appearing too noticeable spending most of her time in her room.

He had been back two days before he knocked on her door.

Sarah had caught him in the kitchen and challenged him..

."Jane told you she was pregnant, didn't she? She's 9 weeks now, there isn't much time to do it safely . What are you going to do to help. ?"

"Oh, oh god,yes, I did ask Marina, she gave me a number, I've got it somewhere" he patted his jeans pockets, "'I'll have to look for it":

"Yes you bloody well will you bastard" Sarah was fuming "This is like urgent you know, and you bloody forgot, you go and find it now you selfish sod, that poor girl , you owe it to her to talk to her at least"

"Hey cool it" mumbled Gideon but he had the decency to look a bit discomfited.

He went up to his room and some time later he came down stairs and knocked on Jane's door. Sarah and Jane were sitting on the bed , surrounded by books, attempting to work but really discussing what might happen next. Gideon opened the door:

"Can I come in ? I've got that number, a Spanish woman, Marina says, very nice, a waitress at the Trattoria , she's helped a few people. Charges £25 ."

Sarah took the paper from him and left the room.

"Alright Janey?" said Gideon.

Jane could not bear to look at him, she kept her eyes down fixed on his legs in faded jeans, she felt foolish, angry, awkward, sad, she felt in such an awful muddle , she still loved him, how could she not, being with him made her feel alive and exhilarated but in her heart she knew it was hopeless, the only thing would be to keep some dignity.

" Yes, its ok sorry about all this " she said bravely letting him off the hook

" Ah sweet Janey " Gideon murmured, reaching for her, this was too much for Jane's fragile self control, she threw herself into his arms and sobbed .

After a few minutes of Gideon patting her on the back she became aware of his body stiffening, withdrawing from her , her heightened sensibility knew he was impatient to be gone from such a messy scene. It was only really then that she knew he did not care for her at all, that she had to cut him out of her heart as his baby was cut out of her body.

Sarah got some money from Davey and she and Jane found the rest. Sarah fixed an appointment with the Spanish woman Marina knew of for a few days time. . The night before they talked about what might happen,

"Are you sure?" Sarah asked, " Sure This is what you want?"

Jane had realised over these difficult weeks something about herself, that within herself she had reserves of strength and determination. There was no point in thinking of a baby, yes one day she would have babies but she did not want to let her parents down and most importantly she did not want to leave Uni, she needed to finish her degree, studying was so important to her . Dreams of bringing up a baby alone were foolish. She said all this to Sarah who looked at her with a new respect. Sarah was used to thinking of herself as the one who took charge in their friendship but Jane was growing up, was becoming more certain . Next morning, skipping breakfast as instructed they set off to the Spanish woman's flat.

She was a warm plump woman called Celine in her 30s black haired and wearing a tight red and yellow dress. She looked at Jane and said straight away:

"You are nervous darling but it will be fine, just like a bad period. Everything will be as before. Aren't you lucky you have your friend with you, some poor girls have to find me on their own."

As she made her preparations she and Sarah talked about a woman's right to choose, a new slogan that was everywhere.

' We need to have control of our reproductive systems" said Sarah," not be at the mercy of unwanted pregnancies "

Jane sniffed and nodded as she climbed up onto the towel covered table. She held tight to Sarah's hand , so grateful for Sarah's calm acceptance and matter of factness about what was taking place . Sarah looked away, Jane squeezed her eyes shut, Celine murmured soothing words. Time passed, an eternity, a minute, a sharp pain and it was over.

"There you are love, now pop your knickers on and go home. Have a nice hot bath and go to bed with a hot drink and you will start in a couple of hours. Take aspirin if the pain is bad. Lots of luck."

"Sweetheart, we'll get a taxi, I told Davy it was more than it was so we can buy some wine as well and celebrate."

At that Jane let out a choked howl.

 "Sarah ,Sarah, I don't want to celebrate I just want to forget all about it"

Sarah stopped stock still and put her arms round Jane and hugged her tight.

"Shhh Shhhhh, it's all over, it will be fine, it will be fine I promise."
"

Later that night what was Jane's and Gideon's baby broke loose and was flushed down the toilet. Only 10 weeks, tiny thing. Sarah slept with Jane that night and the next. Leon knew something was up but did not ask. Paul stayed with Jane during the day when Sarah went to her lectures.It was him she felt she could really talk about how wretched she felt. Paul would just lie beside her, rolling spliffs and gently agreeing with whatever she said. Davy brought some limp daffodils, bought at the end of the day from the Station flower seller which he proffered to her with a joint .Leon left poetry books outside her door. Of Gideon there was no sign.

When Sarah got up on the second morning to go to class Jane got up too.

"I'm fine " she said " I did this so I could get my degree , I don't want to miss anything"

She pushed her books and files into her big orange bag, then shoved in a packet of sanitary towels. The bleeding was quite heavy,but ok, and followed Sarah out into the kitchen .

Leon was there

 "Tea?' he asked ,looking closely at her.

"Yes please " said Jane "You Sarah ?"

Life at St. Agnes Avenue resumed its usual pattern though with exams looming and the occupation which was being planned for the Art School there were not many occasions when they were all in the house together. On one of those Gideon arrived with an Indian take away, enough for them all. He reminded them that before Easter they had agreed to do their very last Ranters gig a big bash in May, just before the exams started, finals for Gideon, Leon, Paul and Howard .

" It will be the last time we all play together and the girls, " he said, looking particularly at Jane." After June I guess we will go our separate ways, hey who knows but let's go out with a bang eh?'

"Yes " said Sarah " absolutely not with a whimper" she too looked at Jane who summoned a smile. Really thought Sarah, she is looking better.

Paul said, "O man, cannot believe we are nearly done, nearly finished, the bands the best thing in my life"

Gideon clapped Paul on the back

" Yeah, cool," he said .

They all talked at once, deciding on a couple of rehearsals and beginning to thrash out favourite songs to play. Marina wandered in and with narrow fingers picked up the leftovers from the nearest plate

" What's the date?" she said."I'm going to Paris again in May "

A sick feeling clutched Jane' s heart, last term she would have been so thrilled and excited to know that Marina might be away and Gideon might come to her. Now she felt cold and embarrassed, she could not imagine lying face to face on her bed with him ever again. But oh, how she wanted to , that was the thing she could not bury,no matter how Sarah-like she tried to be . She loved Gideon, he did not love her , but what did that matter, she could love him, hope still maybe?

Chapter 8: The final gig

Two weeks after her abortion Jane was still feeling wobbly, bleeding had stopped more or less and she was glad to no longer have sore nipples and breasts. Her mood fluctuated from elation, problem solved, life goes on, fueled by more drink than she was used to and more dope, assiduously supplied by Paul or Davy and depression, when she found it hard to concentrate on her work or to summon the energy to get up and go to class.

A date was fixed for a rehearsal for the final gig. Marina had done some startling posters, inspired by stuff she had collected in Paris: covered with slogans in bigger and bigger type *beneath the pavement the beach! Be realistic, demand the impossible! It is forbidden to forbid!* and then their name ,The Ranters ,The Final Gig is the biggest type of all. Marina had not been around much since Easter, but she'd caught Jane in the kitchen one morning and said :

"Everything cool now Jane? Celine sorted you out?" Jane blushed and mumbled "Yes ,thank you" and Marina said

" Well, I guess sweet little Janey's grown up a bit' and left the room bearing a cup of tea.

Jane clutched her chest,that was what Gidcon called her! They must have been talking about her. Gideon had never come to her, to ask if she was ok. In fact he was clearly avoiding her. But she did understand, he hated mess, he hated emotional scenes. That was what Paul said ,what she knew for herself. It was Marina who was the bitch in it all.

When she repeated the conversation, if you could call it that, to Sarah, she was impatient.

"Oh Jane, maybe she did want to know you were ok? At least she asked, which is more than Gideon has done, he just behaves as if nothing has happened."

After that Jane avoided talking to Sarah about her complicated feelings. Paul became her main confidante, Paul understood, listened and did not criticise Gideon. He thought Jane was noble and brave, had made a sacrifice for Gideon and had done the only and best thing. Sarah still sometimes came to her room for a late night drink but instead of light hearted gossip as in the past Sarah seemed to Jane to spend all her time slagging men off, berating Jane for being too submissive, for having low self esteem and even for being anti-women. She left pamphlets about the Abortion Campaign and books ,The Female Eunuch being a favourite. Kitchen arguments now tended to be Davy and Gideon,when he was there,against Sarah with Leon maintaining a more impartial position.

"At least you're prepared to read the books that mean a lot to me," said Sarah to Leon after one bitter argument about priorities for political action. What Davy insisted on calling "The Woman Question" should be left until after the revolution agreed the other two men. All in all the household was fragmenting. Paul was drinking more than ever, he kept a bottle of tequila by his cupboard mattress. He brooded about the end of the band, and the end of the year. His hero would be leaving Brighton, he would no longer have the identity and camaraderie that the band gave him. Would just be Paul from the Valleys again. His shoulder, that the policeman had batoned at the anti vietnam war demo,still troubled him and he took painkillers before their gigs, drumming put quite strain on the shoulder. And Davy and Gideon were doing a lot of speed to help with their revision. Leon was keeping his head down, he suspected some of what had passed with Jane but did not want to intrude. Each of them was locked in their own concerns but, at Gideons urging, they met to rehearse and somehow retrieved some of the energy and glow they had had eight months before .

After their final rehearsal they left the hall laughing, faithful Howard loaded the instruments into the van, helped by Leon. He hadn't seen much of Jane since the start of term, there had been no rehearsals and he had had his head down cramming for finals.

He looked up as she came out of the hall, swinging hands with Paul. She was thinner than before, her hair lank and a few small spots grazed her cheeks.

" Is Jane ok?' he asked Leon

" Oh she's stressed about her exams, I think she had a bit of flu or something"said Leon .

The night of the final gig had been set for May 10th. The week before news had come through from Paris of a huge demo at the Sorbonne, 590 people had been arrested. The barricades were going up. Gideon was determined to go over and film some more of the action, material which he hoped would make his name and get him a foot in at the BBC. Marina just wanted to be wherever it was cool. They decided to leave after the gig, go straight to London on the last train and catch the first morning boat train to Paris . In London, Hornsey Art School ,where Davy had a friend who was one of the organisers of the occupation, was boiling over. He and Sarah decided they would catch that last train too, hang out at The Roundhouse and see what was happening. Everything was in ferment, London, Paris, Berlin, students were leading the action. In

Paris the workers had joined the students ,revolution was in the air. Later when they were alone Jane asked

" What about your exams Sarah?"

"oh I've thought about it but Davy persuaded me , one last bash in London before we really get down and sweat it out ..its ok, I'm on top of my work"

Jane was envious, envious that Sarah felt confident about the exams...she either revised feverishly until 1 or 2 a.m or slumped unable to do anything, totally unable to concentrate, chewing her hair and smoking absently, she was envious that Sarah and Davy had the energy for London . She knew she would have to really key herself up, to give their last gig all she´d got

   She felt desexed , her body separate from her, her mind drifted, swerved,sank.   At the rehearsal Gideon had been sharp

"Come on Janey, move yourself ...you can rock, do it !"

 Sarah and Marina were good, moving together in a rare unity and eventually she had managed to find, deep inside, the joy she'd felt during the 6 months they'd played together when sometimes, Marina away, she and Gideon would leave together and make love and he'd call her his sweet little Janey .

 The night of the final gig there was a big crowd at The Hope, The Ranters regular venue. It was a warm evening, May blossomed and so did the girls in long floral skirt ,little lace vests, every where long hair, boys and girls,interchangeable rainbow kaleidoscopes of beautiful skin, hair, shimmering clothes, embroidery, leather and lace. There was a hint of summer in the air. The exams were still a couple of weeks away, everyone was out to have a good time and give The Ranters a roaring send off. The word was out that Gideon and Marina were off to Paris to help man the barricades which added a sophisticated edge to the night.

Some first years were standing in a huddle outside the pub, waiting for the band to arrive, staring hungrily, nudging each other as the band tumbled out of Howard's van. Jane had a flash of memory, she was back to the night a year ago, when she and Sarah first saw Gideon play solo, tormenting his piano, going back to his place, meeting Leon, Paul, Davy, Marina for the first time. A year ago, she had never smoked a spliff, never sat up all night ,never made love, never been tormented with jealousy, she felt weary, worldly and experienced but at the same time excited as a child.   As ever, Howard was there, pleased to see Jane, hair shiny, eyes unnaturally bright. She had confided in Paul earlier in the evening that she didn't know how she was going to get through the night , she and Sarah had been getting ready together, wriggling in to the bizarre red tube dresses Marina had made for the three of them. They were some weird stretchy fabric she had got in France and, with black knee high boots and black boas, made the girls look vampishly vampiric. Sarah was jollying her along , they were taking swigs of Paul's tequila, who was sitting on Sarah's bed , rolling a spliff and he said
" Here Jane ,have one of these pills, you'll start flying you'll see"
 Before Sarah could saying anything Jane had taken it and swallowed it down with a swift swig of tequila. Almost immediately her limbs felt looser, she gave Paul a huge smile "yeah

Jane, cool, go for it" beamed Paul .

Sarah looked anxiously at Jane "OK love?" she said

"yes yes let's go!! " replied Jane

And now they were arriving at the pub. Jane had no idea how long had passed since they were all in her room, she just knew she felt great, ten feet tall, strong and powerful, she tossed back her hair and sauntered past the gaggle of girls at the door, swinging her boa over her shoulder.

"Go for it Jane" whispered Paul, Sarah squeezed her hand and they exchanged radiant smiles.

The gig went past in a blur, Paul, brilliant drummer that he was,excelled himself, he must have been really pilled up, he hit his drums as if he wanted to tear out the heart of sound, Gideon led and followed him on the piano, dripping sweat on to the keys. Marina,Sarah and Jane moved as one ,and their harmonies were perfect. Gideon kept flashing them all smiles and even taciturn Leon had a thin grin on his face as they played *Jumping Jack Flash* . The crowd went wild, Davey improvised on his rhythm guitar, swirling it round his body like the lead singer of The Who. Later Paul's drum solo in *Born to be Wild* was almost out of control. Paul loved the band and his drums more than anything. Small, shy Paul was a conquering hero behind his kit. He played and played, everyone was stamping their feet ,shouting. Gideon was beginning to look pissed off as he could not get in, finally Leon sidled over, still playing and whispered something to Paul who seemed to come out of a trance and finally gave the tune back to the rest of them. Sarah and Jane exchanged glances but Jane laughed and danced over to kiss Paul lightly on the cheek.

They took a break, had been playing for 40 minutes, drinks were thrust at them ,the noise was huge, Jane heard snatches, could only watch mouths opening and shutting

" Paris tomorrow"   " Paul went crazy" "I loved the poster" "who is Gideon?" "Roundhouse" "Pissed out of his mind" " Have one of these" "Got a fag?"

She felt at the centre of the universe but at the same time she floated above on the ceiling watching her tiny self .She smiled around, at Howard and his mates, at dear Sarah, at darling Paul whose fair hair was dripping with sweat. Leon looked at her anxiously, "OK Jane? Great crowd" he said

"Heavenly bliss" beamed Jane ,taking a long swig of the vodka and orange that magically had appeared in her hand.

The second half was even better, they played *The House of The Rising Sun, Baby Light my Fire*, three of Gideon's songs, one by Paul and as a finale Dylan's *It Aint me Babe* which they encored twice more with the whole pub singing along. What a night!

Then it was all a muddle, packing up, pushing and shoving through the reluctantly dispersing crowd of drunk, stoned and sweaty students. Someone had called a taxi to get Sarah, Davy Gideon and Marina to the station for the last train to London. Howard was loading the gear into the van helped by Paul and Leon. Suddenly, as they waved goodbye to the taxi Jane felt weird, she was drunk she knew that and giddy ,she rocked on her feet,

"Sit down Jane," said Howard. " As soon as I'm done I'll take you home."

Leon and Paul said they were going on to a party , they both kissed an almost comatose Jane, who was slumped on a low wall,

"I'm ok" she mumbled to Pauls' query " heavenly bliss"

Paul was incandescent , the speed, the tequila, the beers and the joy of performing had flown Paul up to heaven, his feet hardly touched the ground, his pupils were huge and his smile stretched from ear to ear.

"'See you later then babe" he said, wrapping her in his skinny arms. .

Howard drove her to ST. Agnes Avenue, he helped her out of the van and took her up to her room, she fell on the bed almost straight away, passed out. Howard covered her with a blanket and stood, irresolute, looking at her. After a bit he went out, closing the door softly and drove off to find the party .

Chapter 9: The Aftermath

Jane woke up feeling like death, she had a horrible taste in her mouth and her head was pounding. She dragged herself out of bed and looked in the mirror. Her eyes were red and puffy, her hair tangled. She groaned out loud, God what a mess she thought. She went along to the bathroom. Of course, most of the house were away, she could have a long bath, wash her hair. First she went into the kitchen and swallowed a couple of aspirin and 2 glasses of water in quick succession. Feeling marginally better she collected her towel and went to grapple with the bathroom geyser. Half an hour later she emerged, pulled on some jeans and a sweater and went into the kitchen to make some coffee. She put on the kettle and while she was waiting for it to boil she put some bread under the grill to toast. For the first time she looked at her watch, it was mid day, Paul would probably be stirring in his cupboard, so after she had eaten her toast and drunk down her coffee she decided to make him some, together they could talk about the night before .She wondered about the party he and Leon had gone to, had they come back even? She pushed at the door of his cupboard, God it smelt in there

" Hey, Paul, wake up, it's practically afternoon" she said, peering in at his tumbled form.

"Paul, Paul" she looked closer, there was vomit around his mouth, his trusty bottle of tequila was lying on its side by his head.

"Paul" she screamed, shaking him, he did not move ,was inert and floppy, smelt dreadful. Jane screamed, and screamed again,

"Paul!Help! Leon help, someone come please, please" she was sobbing, shaking Paul, screaming.

 Leon appeared, half dressed. He took one look then:

"Leave him, Janey." He said gently " Go upstairs and knock on Miss Pink's door. Ask her to phone an ambulance. Quickly, pull yourself together"

Jane stood up and rushed upstairs. It was Saturday, luckily Miss Pink was in. She took one look at Jane, put her arms around her and said

" Deep breaths girl, slow down ,breathe, now tell me what has happened". Incoherently Jane gasped,

"Its Paul, please phone an ambulance, I think he's dead ,oh hurry please, please"

Miss Pink acted quickly, she phoned, briskly gave the details then thrust a glass of brandy at Jane.

" Who is with him dear?'she asked

" Leon" said Jane.

" Now, you stay here dear, just lie on the couch while I go and help Leon, the ambulance will be here any minute "

" No no don't leave me" wailed Jane following Miss Pink downstairs .

Leon had wiped Paul's mouth,was desperately pumping his chest, breathing into his mouth. He looked up as they women appeared

" It's no good," he said somberly.

He looked appallingly young, his cool detached persona stripped away, raw grief and fear scrawled over his face .

The rest of the day time was distorted ,sometimes agonisingly slow and then oddly speeded up. Leon and Jane went in the ambulance to the hospital with Paul's body but he was pronounced dead on arrival. Then they were interviewed by the police who came back to the house. They examined Paul's cupboard, his vomit stained mattress, asked about the previous night, Leon said Paul had been drinking heavily, he did not mention all the pills and coke that Paul had had at the party. He remembered them coming home together around 3a.m Paul falling onto his mattress laughing and shushing and waving his tequila bottle. Leon, also for him, rather drunk, had gone up to his room and left Paul to sleep. They said that some time in the night he had been sick, choked on his own vomit.

Leon left Jane with Miss Pink and went round to fetch Howard. Miss Pink, when she saw how distraught and panicky Jane was, called her doctor who came and gave her some pills so she could sleep. Miss Pink tucked her up in her own room, understanding Jane could not be downstairs. Once she was sleeping and the police had finished she went down and cleared out Paul's cupboard, throwing the mattress out. When Howard arrived he took charge, the horror was contacting Paul's parents and aunt, Howard did that and Howard dealt with the police's further questions, with the undertaker who took away the body, he brought in food which they could not eat. Jane could not stop crying, she was exhausted, clung to Leon

" It is my fault, if I had looked in on him earlier, if I had not been so drunk I can't bear it its all my fault"

Leon and Howard did not know how to cope, when she wasn't crying, Jane sat huddled on Leon´s bed staring at the wall.

Sarah and Davy arrived back very late on Sunday night and crashed in Sarah's room so it was not until Monday morning that they learned what had happened.

Jane moved down from Leon´s room to be with Sarah but it was not like being with Leon, they had been through the terrible business together. She went over and over finding the body, cried and said how Paul had been her best friend, was the only person who understood how she felt about Gideon. The abortion and Paul's death were all muddled together,she kept saying " It's my punishment" After three days of this, Jane not eating and crying Howard said to Sarah

"I'm going to ring her parents and take her back home," Sarah was at the end of her tether, she could not cope with Jane, with all her guilt feelings, she was trying to study but Jane's presence lying listlessly on her bed distracted her and made her feel uneasy . She was desperately worried and did not know how to help her friend. Marina and Gideon were due back from Paris and she thought that would only make Jane worse, so she agreed. She took a passive inert Jane to the doctor who arranged that, in the circumstances, she could have an aegrotat for her exams and have sick leave until the autumn.

 Four days after the glory of The Ranters final gig Howard drove Jane back to Shropshire in a state of total collapse, her year that had begun with such thrills was over.

Two days later Gideon arrived back from Paris. Dumping his rucksac onto the hall floor he burst into the kitchen
"Hi, anyone in? " he shouted.
The house was quiet, he went back out into the hall, looked up the stairs. He noticed Paul's cupboard door was shut, idly, unthinkingly, he opened it , stared in surprise at the empty space, no mattress ,no tequila bottle . Footsteps came running down the stairs, it was Leon.
"Hi, whats with this? said Gideon, "has Paul gone?"

Leon looked at him: " Yes, am afraid he has gone, I'm sorry but he's dead, choked on his own vomit, the night of the last gig, when you were on the way to Paris "

" Jesus! Shit, oh man, Shit! No" said Gideon in horror.

He and Leon stared at each other

" God what happened, who?'

Leon cut across him, "Jane found him late on Saturday morning, she's gone home, she is in a bad way been given an agroetat for the exams,"

"Poor Jane , Jesus that must have been heavy, fuck, fuck, I can't believe it, man ,oh Paul, he was such a brilliant drummer, such a sweet guy" Gideon's voice shook.

The two of them wandered into the kitchen, Leon opened some beers and started to fill Gideon in on all that had happened. He sat in a state of shock, quiet for him, Sarah and Davy came in, they had both been in the library revising. The four of them sat up late, talking about Paul, going over what had happened. Sarah and Davy telling of the shock when they got back, how strong Howard had been, Miss Pink's calm helpfulness, the police, the agony of talking to Paul's family. They smoked some spliffs, Gideon rallied and began to talk about Paris, the General strike.

"Where is Marina? " asked Sarah eventually .

". Oh she decided to stay in Paris, it's all kicking off, she says she's not going back to the art school. I was tempted myself, its revolution there ,but the bloody exams, had to come back" Gideon,

ambitious and focused, knew he had to get his degree if he wanted to achieve his ambitions, but he'd brought back lots of great footage from Paris and was planning on editing it over the summer.
"We are talking about going to California later, fantastic scene there, San Francisco, Marina has some connections there, her mum lives in the US" Gideon trailed off, Sarah and Davy exchanged a look
"Wow" said Davy . Leon kept silent, and Sarah said " Always where the action is eh?"

Just before the exams started the five of them, Howard ,Sarah, Davy ,Gideon and Leon travelled in Howard´s van to Paul's funeral in the Welsh valleys. Jane had begged her parents to let her go but she was still in a very disturbed state and the family doctor would not allow it. She sent Leon a short poem, a haiku, she had written about Paul, one night when they were lying on her bed talking about Gideon, it was full of love for her friend and she asked Leon if he could perhaps give it to his parents.
The day before an enormous wreath of lilies arrived at the house "What the fuck?' said Davy, taking it from the delivery man and coming into the kitchen where the others were drinking coffee, Gideon sighed, "Oh I rang Marina at her father´s to tell her, she must have sent them" sure enough there was a card which said 'Goodbye to a great drummer.' Sarah said "Well that's rather nice but it is going to take up half the bloody van, Typical"
"I suppose we should take them, can be from all of us, we hadn't thought about a wreath , people do bring wreaths, a sign of respect I

think" said Leon

Only Leon had been to a funeral before, his father's when he was just a little boy. Sarah insisted they ought to wear black. Howard of course had a dark suit and tie but Gideon and Davy were in skin tight black jeans, black sweat shirts and leather jackets, Davy's with long fringes. Gideon had a long red and black scarf round and round his neck. Leon was dressed from head to toe in black, loose black shirt and waistcoat. Sarah had found a vintage droopy black dress and she wore a black bolero also fringed. The boys tied back their long hair and when the four of them looked at each other, in spite of the painful occasion they could not help laughing. "Paul would have been so tickled" said Sarah with tears in her eyes.

Davy gave her a quick hug and they went out and piled into Howards van.

As they drove into Maerdy, at the head of the Rhonda Valley, they looked out at the rows of miners' cottages, terrace after terrace of little houses , marching up the valley with slag heaps and pit workings looming over them. . They exchanged looks, none of them had been to the valleys, this was the narrow world Paul had flown from with his brains and his drumsticks. They drove around looking for the chapel, silently taking in the scene. Finally they found it "Quick, go past" said Gideon, showing a surprising empathy

"We don't want to park the van by the hearse" The van had THE RANTERS stencilled on the side and a cartoon of Felix the Cat smoking a spliff , Gideon was right, they needed to tuck it out of sight. They climbed out, Sarah, Davy and Leon had been squashed in the back, Gideon had the enormous wreath in the front . They walked self consciously down the road, Sarah , Gideon and the wreath leading the way.

A crowd, all in black, was gathered outside, they all turned to stare. Davy spotted Paul's aunt who all of them had got to know over the year they had lived together. Quickly they joined her and were introduced to the grieving parents . Aunt Vi took the wreath from Gideon and into the chapel which was a great relief. Paul's father said ,formally,

" Thank you all for coming. Paul loved being in the band, he used to say it was the best thing in his life. Which of you is Gideon?"

Gideon stepped forward ,his hand outstretched, Paul's father held it tightly

" He worshipped you, you know" he said.

" I loved him," said Gideon, his posh english voice a contrast to the lilting welsh tones around him,

"We all did" the others murmured their assent " and he was a brilliant musician."

They filed into the chapel, the band all sitting together. The tight knit community stared at these english ,whispering and speculating about them .

The service was unbearably moving, a male voice choir sang, Gideon spoke, briefly and with heart, about Paul's gentleness, his humour, his brilliant drumming .

" Like all great drummers he held us all together" he finished   "We will be lost without him."   Sarah squeezed his hand as he came back to sit beside her, visibly moved. In that moment she forgave him a lot. Leon, with the parents previous agreement, read Jane's short poem. Sarah sobbed, Davy put a comforting arm around her, Howard was glad Jane was not there, it would have been too much for her. They all sat together , the band, no longer an entity without Paul., in grief and regret.

Afterwards the father invited them back to the house. They had noticed how the chapel was mainly filled with men and aunt Vi told them it was the custom for the women to be at home waiting. She encouraged them to come up

"Do come, it would mean a lot to my sister, nobody will bite you" she urged, noticing their hesitation. "They want to know Paul's friends."

They walked with the other mourners up the steep terraced street, Sarah with Aunt Vi, Gideon with a lad who introduced himself as Bryn and had been at school with Paul, Davy, Leon and Howard together. Howard, tall and broad in his formal suit, oddly seemed the most out of place. Once in the house, in the clearly rarely used front room, crammed with people, Sarah joined the other women, her easy friendliness and warmth soon won them over and she helped with cups of tea and passing sandwiches. Quite soon some of the older men moved out into the backyard, drinking beer and smoking. The younger relatives all wanted to talk to the boys, to ask about the band. Again Sarah was surprised at Gideon's thoughtfulness when

she saw he was passing around some photographs of them playing and a lovely one of Paul. He saw Sarah looking and said to her
"Will you give these to Paul's mum?"
"Ofcourse, a nice thing to have done Gids'
The worst moment of the whole day was when Paul's mum came over to them, all standing together now and preparing to leave for the long drive back to Brighton
"Would you like to see Paul's bedroom? " she asked, red eyed and barely holding herself together.
The four band members shuffled up the steep narrow stairs, there were two doors on a small landing, they had already discovered the bathroom was an add-on downstairs, off the kitchen . Howard had chickened out ,so it was just the four of them crowded into the room.
 "He was poorly a lot as a boy, the asthma, had to spend quite a lot of time up here in bed, missing school, he used to listen to the radio and all the time be banging out the rhythms on a tray until we bought him his drum kit. The drum kit took up most of the room, there was a desk on one wall, a window looked out onto the mountain. The walls were covered with posters of his favourite bands, and some Ranters posters. The four of them stood awkwardly, all of them uncomfortable in the face of her pain. It was Leon who spoke, years of supporting his depressive mother gave him a mature sensibility, He put his arm around her frail shoulders
" We are all so sorry for your loss, for your pain and thank you for welcoming us and showing us his room.
"Now" he looked at the others, " We will have another side to

remember, and we will never forget him, rest assured" The others all said what they could, Sarah holding back tears and squeezing the mother's hand tight, they were all so young, facing the reality and finality of the loss of one of their own . Quiet and subdued they said their goodbyes and left the small house full of grief .

Paul's funeral was the last time they were all together. The boys took their finals, then Gideon, with barely a goodbye, went off to California to join Marina. He had edited his Paris film and his parents had given him the money to buy his own decent camera. He was planning a documentary on the Summer of Love. He had ruthlessly moved on, with Paul's death, music was behind him, a better vehicle for his ambition was film. It was left to the others, minus Jane, to dismantle the house in St Agnes Avenue. Sarah cried when they carried out Paul's old armchair, bald on the arms where he had endlessly drummed to the music that played in the evenings. Leon took down the posters from the walls, carefully putting them in the boxes with his other stuff.

Sarah went to stay with Jane and then to France with her family. In September she and Jane started their 3rd year. They found a flat together. Jane, determined to throw herself into her work and make a new start. She worked hard all that year, wrote a lot of poetry, got a First in her finals. Sarah got heavily into feminist politics ,she had an old school friend at Warwick University studying English whose tutor was Germaine Greer. Sarah went to visit several times, sat at the feet of this amazing woman , drinking in her radical way of seeing the world. . She threw herself into campaigns and decided that she would study law after her degree.

Davy, to his own and everyone else's surprise, had got a decent degree and had discovered ,somewhat belatedly , a passion for sociology. He had decided to aim for an academic career, after all, teaching was another form of showing off. He embarked on an MA, so was also still in Brighton. He moved into Marina's old room at the Trip Out Cafe. Sarah and Jane used to meet him there regularly and sometimes they would go to gigs. Dancing with Sarah, Jane reclaimed some of her old self.

Leon came down to visit a couple of times. He had gone back home to Sheffield, like them all deeply shaken by events. He had decided to go traveling, in Asia, and was working in his old factory to save money . Jane sometimes sent him poems.

And then Howard, who was now working for a finance company in London but who came to Brighton frequently, asked Jane to marry him. Tired, not knowing what to do, regretting her abortion, longing for the lost baby, missing Paul, Jane agreed, a safe haven with Howard, marriage, motherhood, no more wild highs and lows. Sarah tried to talk her out of it but her parents were delighted, having been so worried about their only daughter and her brothers were pleased. It was the easy option and Jane took it with a mixture of relief and shame.

Chapter 10: Varanasi ,India 1972

It was the cow dust hour, Leon's favourite time of day . The burning sun was slipping into the muddy Ganges, the usual cacophony of cow bells, rickshaws, car horns was subsiding into a background murmur. A few of the faithful were still carefully picking their way down the steps of the ghats to bathe. Marigolds and tiny clay pots of lights were bobbing about on the water. He could hear the glorious sound of bhavans, holy chants, from the priests across at the burning ghats, helping the dead on their way. He gazed and gazed, weary from the heat, he tried to empty his mind, to still the monkey mind as he had been taught up in the Himalayas. Today was momentous, he had finally bought his plane ticket home .The two years he had spent roaming the subcontinent were coming to an end and it was time he thought of his future.

A movement to his left brought him out of his reverie. He became aware of someone sitting next to him on the steps, he noticed slim brown feet, toe rings,an ankle bracelet. So far so typical of female western travelers he took a glance up and noticed a tangle of red pre-raphaelite hair hanging over a face. That hair, who? Where? As he turned to look properly the young woman lifted her head, shook back her hair and stared straight at him through almond shaped green eyes flecked with gold, red rimmed but still arresting .

"Hi Leon" Of course, he recognised the soft throaty voice

"Christ! Marina! What the hell are you doing here?"

They stared at each other and then she put a thin grubby hand on his knee, it was faintly trembling.

"Same as you I suppose . I saw you the other day. Do you live here?"

" Sort of. I have a room, been here a few weeks "

"So can I stay ?' she asked

O God thought Leon. All the stuff he had tried to forget about the days in that student house came flooding back. Of course, Marina and Gideon had missed all the horror, they had been in Paris. Returned to a house in shock, in mourning. Paul's death, Jane's suicide attempt , they had been oblivious of it all.

Marina did not even come to Paul's funeral. He had a sudden memory of Gideon, subdued for once muttering in answer to Sarah's indignant question that Marina would not come back from Paris. He had never liked Marina, too self absorbed, too selfish, unkind to Jane, disdainful of all of them. She came and went in the house, Gideon her official lover but Davey too he had suspected. He kept his distance from her, like all of them he was fascinated but he was repelled in equal measure. Her disregard for everyone's feelings making her toxic as far as he was concerned. Especially her cruelty to poor Jane.

He realised that Marina's hand was gripping his knee

"Please" she said and was that a hint of desperation in her voice? What had happened to arrogant imperious Marina? He looked more closely at her. She looked drawn, her classically beautiful features had an unhealthy sheen, the hand on his knee was like a claw. She was much too thin. Hippy disease, he thought, dehydration, dysentery, hepatitis, opium, heat, malaria..any or all of these or just India.

"O.k just a couple of days though. It's a very small room" Leon said reluctantly

'lets go"

He guessed something had happened to the usually aloof Marina . Reticent himself he was reluctant to probe but for old times sake, damsel in distress he rationalised to himself, whatever this strange unlikely encounter would bring it was time limited he was off in a few days . He got up and Marina who he now saw had been propping herself up on a big carpet bag dragged herself to her feet. As they walked away from the ghats Leon became aware of a tall barefoot westerner, with matted hair wearing a sarong and swaying under the influence of god knew what.

"Fuck off then you fucking English bitch " he shouted after them. Marina, summoning vestiges of her remembered arrogance, turned and gave him the finger.

"It's nobody, Hans, an idiot I was travelling with" she said by way of explanation as usual with her, remembered Leon, no explanation at all. So, I am a better bet than dirty Hans, he thought, typical of Marina in her hour of need, had wasted no time in ditching one man and battening on to another .

The first two nights and days Marina stayed in the room which he had thoroughly cleaned and organised when he had first moved in, slept, only waking to drink the water he put beside the bed and to sometimes have a few spoonfuls of rice. She slept on the bed and Leon borrowed a charpoy from his landlord which he could just squeeze in at the foot of the bed. The rusty fan whirred and Marina tossed and turned, muttering occasionally in french, sometimes shouting incoherently. Leon mopped her brow and helped her to the filthy toilet shared by 6 others in the little lodgings . On day three her fever broke and she surfaced wild eyed and hungry.

"Where can I get clean ?" She asked, her first coherent words since arriving in the spartan room. Leon showed her to the basic shower in the cramped bathroom and after what seemed hours she emerged, wild wonderful hair washed and stark naked . Leon took one look and said angrily

" For God's sake get dressed and we will go and get something to eat, I'll wait outside"

While he waited he mused on what India did to westerners. Marina had clearly succumbed to the heat, the food and the dirt , like so many others had probably smoked too much cheap dope, drunk Bhang to cool down, the cannabis infused lhassi that travelers knocked back as if it was beer. A deeply different and deeply weird hit awaited too much consumption of any of the highs that Mother India offered these thirsty western children who unaccountably had started to roam her vast and varied land.

He tried to remember what he had last heard about Marina. Certainly he did not remember her ever expressing any desire to go to India.

Whereas he, sickened by politics and the increasing violence of the demos, desperate for a change after the things that had happened at

St Agnes Avenue, focused his attention on getting to what he thought would be a more spiritual place, somewhere with totally different energy from the corrupt and individualist west. In 1970, after a year's hard graft in a factory at home in Sheffield Leon had taken off and for the last two years he had been travelling. First in Iran, Afghanistan then India, Dharamsala, Rishikesh, Hardwar, in the Himalayas, keeping close to Mother Ganges. He criss-crossed the subcontinent hitching, 3rd class trains, roofs of buses. . During those years he read voraciously, in Hinduism, Buddhism, Jainism. He picked up some Hindi and smatterings of Urdu. He spent 6 months in a monastery in Dharmkot where he learned meditation and sat at the feet of a Teacher, a round and cheerful monk, Rinpoche Lim. But the master saw the pupil was a man to be in the world and sent him on his way. He lived for some months with a jolly Yorkshire girl called Molly, whom he had met on the bus. She was a hopeful, optimistic and down to earth northerner. She was an antidote to the rarefied ascetic path he was in danger of following. It was she who had introduced him to teaching. She helped in an ashram school in Hardwar talked him into coming along between meditations and he found he enjoyed it and for the first time since coming to India felt a sense of purpose. They parted on good terms and he with gratitude. Of the many encounters he had with other travelers, with Sadhhus, those with Indian musicians were the most important. He had kept up his music, traveled with his guitar and sat whenever he could alongside the sitar players. The different scale, the improvised way of playing, the holy attitude to the music touched Leon powerfully. Yes, he would miss India profoundly but now he was ready to return to England and to make another life. And real life had abruptly intruded in the person of Marina, a disturbing blast from the past.

During the year he was saving he had gone down to Brighton a couple of times, mainly to see Jane and Sarah . Davy had stayed on in Brighton, he had kept in touch with Gideon who, on the strength of his Paris 68 film and some footage from California had got a place as a graduate trainee at the BBC .

Lucky sod. None of them knew where Marina was, she had dropped out of the Art School, gone to California . The only one who might know was Gideon and he was not saying. Pride maybe, Leon had thought, then perhaps she had dumped him. It was February, he had left for India on his birthday, Feb 20th so it must have been at the beginning of the month. It was bitterly cold as seaside towns can be, the sea was sullen and grey. The three of them had an Indian meal in honour of his departure. Afterwards back at Sarah and Janes flat they talked mainly of India and his plans. Davy was really focussing on his work. Sarah had said she might do law after her finals, she was even more involved in feminist politics. Jane did not say much, she looked so much better though, hair shiny and had put on some weight. But there was a bewildered wary look deep in her eyes, Leon had studied her covertly. She would be alright he had thought, but not for a while yet. They drank, had a few farewell spliffs and the evening ended, no resolution, how could there be, but a sort of peace between them.

The door opened and Marina finally emerged, she was wearing a sleeveless white cheesecloth top and a white skirt, actually a sari petticoat but he guessed she did not know that. She had a necklace of big turquoise stones and turquoise sandals. She looked fantastic, in spite of the standard hippy chick gear, Marina managed, as always, to look utterly individual and aloof.

Leon stirred and got up from the ground where he had been squatting outside the door, lost in thoughts of the past.

"Come on then, I know a small place not far where we can eat" Marina walked silently beside him. As always in Varanasi the streets were heaving with life. Leon led as they wove their way through narrow streets, every now and then a shrine, smeared with paint and hung with the ubiquitous marigolds. Crowds going about their mysterious business, they passed men carrying huge bundles of washing, an old fellow on a wobbly bike festooned with more plastic buckets than seemed possible hanging from the handlebars and back carrier. They all looked at Marina, covertly and openly, astonished by her hair and her regal bearing. A couple of westerners stumbled past, one laughing uproariously. It was a relief to dive through a hanging plastic curtain into a dark little tea shop.

They did not talk much, drank tea and ate rice and dahl and a pile of brinjal cooked in a delicious spicy sauce. Leon told Marina a bit about his travels, then she volunteered that she had been in India a year, had spent some time in Goa, had wandered to Pondicherry but it was too French she said, had heard about Varanasi, thought she would come and take a look. She glossed over who she had been with and the events which had led to their meeting . They sat for the most part quietly. Marina was clearly ravenous and devoured the food. When they had finished she gave a huge yawn ,showing perfect teeth and said

"I'll pay and then I would like some more sleep"

"OK,thanks.You'e got money?"

" oh I've always got money," Marina said bitterly. "My bastard dad keeps me in funds, to keep me away from his sweet french life and bourgeois french wife and french brats "

Like the others at St. Agnes Avenue Leon had never known anything about Marina's background, so here was a small revelation.

They got to their feet and started for home. Leon wanted to go via the Ghats, maybe there would be some music and he needed to see the Ganges. Aware that his days in India were numbered he wanted as much of the magic as possible. This route was busier, people pushed against them, at one point Marina turned and shouted "Fuck Off" to a dishevelled Sadhu who crowded just too close. As they pushed through the crowds Marina slipped, grabbed hold of Leon "Shit shit shit ,I have trodden in a cow pat, urgh ,it's all over my feet." half sobbing she picked up her foot to look, the hem of her skirt was smeared and cow shit clung to her sandal. Trembling with rage she looked wildly round. A group of westerners squatting on the steps noticed her discomfiture and laughed , a Sadhu came close and muttered something, his garlicky breath spraying her face. She hit out and screamed .Quickly Leon grabbed her arm tightly

" Calm down, nearly back, just calm down, hold on to me, but first we will go down to the river and wash your sandal." Marina held tightly to his arm as they picked their way down, past people seated on the steps, old men, ancient women, skinny half clad children. Some glanced at the angry white woman with the red hair and the tall thin Englishman. Leon could feel Marina's anger through the grip on his arm. She bathed her foot in the muddy water and then turned to him, her face was a mask of fury.

"Get me back you bastard" she said

Leon was taken aback by the fury on her face and her rank ingratitude for all that he had done for her. He took a deep breath and managed to hold back a retort and eventually they reached the sanctuary of his room.

As soon as the door was shut Marina started:

"Fucking India . I hate it, I hate it. Smells of shit, dirty bloody Indians, dirty fucking hippies. Stupid temples , disney bloody land, gods with ten arms and five heads, elephant heads, skulls" she was incandescent with rage, words tumbling out

incoherently

"I hate the beggars, the squalor, the cripples, the fucking cows, dirty dirty...."

She began to sob, resting her head on her knees, crouched on the bed, her hands clutching her flaming hair. She was choking with pain and misery. India was too much for her, it had rejected her so she rejected it .

Leon knew better than to say anything. He sat on the charpoy and waited. After a while her breathing calmed and he offered her water and a piece of wet cloth to wipe her face. Time passed, he breathed in and out , counting the breaths as he had been taught. Quietly breathing Shanti ,shanti, shanti and hoping that would give Marina peace.

Finally Marina sat up , shook back her hair and looked at him. He could not read the expression on her face.

"So you sanctimonious prick, " she said . " Did you enjoy that rundown of your lovely crap India?

" I hated you all you know, you smug lot at ST Agnes Avenue. You, so superior, You and Gideon, all your big words,your politics, the struggle of this and that. You thought you were all so fucking clever, so boring, half the time I didn't know what you were talking about, I learnt fuck all at my wanky progressive schools except how to fuck. You lot though, all so sure of yourselves , so smug. And Davy and his drugs, cocky Sarah and soppy Jane and her poetry and wet little Paul. And he was in love with Gideon you know? Expect you were too, eh Leon. That stupid Jane was and he didn't give a shit.."

Leon roused himself

"That's enough Marina. I do not want to hear this . I am going out. I will come by in the morning to see if you are ok and then on Tuesday I am off to Delhi so you will need to decide what you are going to do. I am sorry you are so angry about everything, it seems the whole world makes you angry. That must be truly horrible for you."

Leon left and went down to the Ghats. Who was this Marina ? She had hated them all? Her words revolved around in his head. She had been the insecure one? Had masked her insecurity in arrogance and her sexuality? He knew from lads at home who he had been at school with how ignorance can quickly turn to aggression, a self protective shell. And Marina's self protection was to present herself as the superior one? Her money and her looks and her otherness had enabled this facade. He knew Jane had been scared of her, that she puzzled Sarah, that Davy was in awe of her. He had kept his distance, always sensing, as the sensitive child of a widowed mother, that there was something reckless and disturbed at her core. The very thing that attracted other men made him wary. With Gideon it was different, he was the star, the front man of the band, he had a boundless confidence, self obsessed himself, he was able to ignore the darkness in Marina's soul, if he was even aware of it.

He had grabbed a shawl as he left the room and wrapping himself up he settled down, leaning wearily against a wall to spend the night watching the river and dozing, not the first time he had done this There were always people about getting on with the myriad small tasks that made up the days and nights of the pilgrims who had come to worship and bury their dead beside Mother Ganga .

Next morning, early, he drank two clay cups of sweet chai from a stall and, buying another one for Marina, wandered back to his room. He wondered what mood Marina would be in but had not expected she would be gone. Her carpet bag was still there and on the bed was a piece of paper, torn from a sketch pad. It was a drawing of the room, with a tumble of clothes on the bed and a blurred outline of a body with red hair spread over the pillow. No face. All the other details of the room were sharp, clothes hanging on hooks on the wall, the rickety table with his tin mug and plate, a pile of books on a little shelf in the corner. her bag, his rucksac, all meticulously drawn. He studied the picture for some time then turning it over he saw the date, his name and the single word, Sorry.

He decided the best thing to do was to wait, she had to come back for her things. He started to sort his stuff. He was off in two days, needed to get a rail ticket, some money, pack up and discard remnants of the life he had lived for two years. He had planned to spend his last day at Sanarth, not far and a peaceful special place. It was here the Buddha had preached his first sermon and Leon found it balm for his soul.

The door opened and Marina came in .

"Hi " she said with a quick glance at his face and then away, to take in his preparations.

"So, when are you off ?'

"Tomorrow but today I thought I would go to Sanarth"

A look Leon could not interpret crossed her face. He realised after a minute it was fear, or at least unease. She was obviously still wobbly.

On an impulse he said "Why don't you come, it is a good place to be still and quiet, no hassles, no cows ? "

This a small acknowledgement of Marinas outburst the night before.

Leon had always been taciturn, he knew when not to speak and his acceptance calmed Marina, there were to be no recriminations which she would have run from, just a quiet acknowledgement .

"Oh and thank you for the picture. it's really good.

I need to go to the station to get a train ticket for Delhi, I´ll take a rickshaw and will be back in an hour or so and then we will get the bus to Sanarth .ok? it's still early so I won't have to wait long"

"Right. Thanks .See you" said Marina.

Leon looked at her,took in the skimpy top and sari under skirt she was wearing.

"Maybe, I don't know, it's a very holy place, maybe wear trousers and cover your arms? That way you wouldn't get hassle on the bus and it would be more fitting. you know? that would be cool" said Leon, a shade nervous at her reaction but she merely nodded and said "See you later"

After some thought Leon bought two tickets to Delhi, third class was cheap enough and if Marina did not want it no doubt someone else would, off their head hippies often hung around the station expecting to buy a ticket in five minutes not factoring in the endless queues and wait lists and all the other ramifications of the glorious Indian railway system. He decided to see how Marina was during the day but he had come to the conclusion it was time she left India before she cracked up completely. The tense and trembling girl he had left at his room was such a far cry from the arrogant aloof Marina of their Brighton days.

They caught a bus the 10 kilometres to Sarnath, managed to get seats and Marina sat quietly beside him. She was wearing loose light blue cotton trousers and a long sleeved yellow cheese cloth shirt and had also pinned up her hair .

With an effort she dragged her gaze from the passing scene and said "So what's the place we are going"

" Long answer or short?" said Leon.

"Long" she said .

Leon intuited that she did not want to think ,wanted distraction from the noise in her head so he began to tell her how Gautama Buddha , after receiving enlightenment at Bodh Gaya, had preached his first sermon at Sanarth , that for thousands of years it had been a holy place with many monasteries and temples until it was savaged sacked and destroyed by the Turks in the 12th Century.

"However ,the good old British in 1910 set up an archeological museum to house all the wonderful findings. There is an Ashoka pillar, all sorts of statues. And in the deer park, where we are going ,there are lots of ruins of stupas ."

Marina had continued to look out of the window but he could tell her attention was on him asked

"What was his first sermon about?"

"Well, the path to Enlightenment, the Four Noble Truths and the Eightfold path"

She turned to look at him, he could see how strained she was, how tense, she seemed to be just holding herself together.

"Do you believe that stuff?

"Well ,"Leon hesitated, "the Buddha's teachings answer a lot of questions for me.."

"What are the four noble truths then"

" Hmm, There is suffering, suffering has a cause, the cause is removable , there are ways to remove it."

Marina sighed, muttered something he could not catch and turned back to the window.

The quietness of the Deer Park worked its magic on Leon as usual, most people, and in those days there were no hordes of visitors, headed for the museum but Leon and Marina wandered past the ruined stupas. Leon indicated a clump of trees .

"I am going over there, will sit for a while, meditate, ok?"

Marina just nodded and wandered off .

Some time later he became aware that she was sitting beside him. He opened his eyes and looked at her. And she began to talk, a stream of words, it was as if a dam had broken and first disjointedly and then more coherently she talked about her life. Her completely disrupted schooling, trailing after her mother, who had left the father she adored when she was 5 , across Europe, every now and then when her mother had a new lover or got fed up with her she was packed off to her father. But her Father was always busy making money, had little time for his increasingly difficult daughter . She was sent off to boarding school in England, expelled, back to Paris, another school.. one thing her parents agreed on was english schooling. A totally disrupted and unhappy childhood.

"one thing about wanky progressive schools is there's always plenty of Art." she said "I spent most of my time in my last two schools in the Art rooms and so that's how I ended up, at the Art School in Brighton. My dad always came across with the money, guilt of course.

And then I met you lot , St Agnes Avenue was the first time I had been around normals" she laughed, a choking sound. "At my schools all the kids were weird, some of them had like three sets of parents, whatever"

During this long monologue Leon had watched her face, saw how difficult she found this disclosure, this was not a narrative to impress or shock but an attempt to make sense of who she was.

"That stuff about suffering having a cause, that made me think about my childhood, my so called parents"

She fell silent.

Leon made no comment but said "That must have been hard to live and to tell"

she looked at him with relief, the last thing she wanted was analysis .

"I think," said Leon, "you should come to Delhi with me tomorrow and get a flight back to Europe. Stay in a nice hotel, you say you have money, and they will book your ticket for you ."

Marina gave a moan…"But I don't know where to go, what to do , everything is meaningless , why go it will be just different shit wherever I am but still shit"

Leon studied her, she was staring at the ground, twisting the threads tied round her wrist, acquired at some temple.

" Well, firstly you can be more comfortable , not tripping over dirty cows and hippies." he smiled gently and took her unresisting hand, "You have a talent for drawing, the picture of my room caught it exactly, the atmosphere as well as the detail. Maybe you could go back to Art School, find some direction. I don't know, Marina but I do not think you should stay here. I think you are still unwell, in mind as well as body"

Tears were running down her face, her body was taut, she held tightly to his hand and took a deep breath .

"Maybe, I don't know."

Leon was silent waiting for her to compose herself. After a while he said

"Well, how about we just live in the moment for now, enjoy being here in this holy place, not think of anything except here and now. Just try and let go of anger and pain'

A tremulous laugh escaped Marina

" How did you get to be so wise then? That flinty eyed marxist has become a bloody guru"

This was better ,a flash of the old sardonic Marina, but the words were said with warmth, not anger and Leon squeezed her hand

"Let's eat something" he said and getting up they went in search of a food stall.

They spent a peaceful day together, not talking much, back in Varanasi Leon took Marina to the very last ghat, it was much quieter there, not many people came to that end. They got some cold beers and Leon played his guitar for a while, a couple of other travellers Leon had played with before were there and the three of them improvised around the chords and riffs. and it was lovely, quiet and peaceful. For the first time Marina saw how beautiful India was, the lights bobbing on the water, the coolness after the stifling heat of the day, the possibilities of the spirit. She drifted in and out of awareness of the present. She made no attempt to connect with the others but this was not disdain but because she was in a world of her own, an empty space was opening in her teeming mind.

Later when they went back to Leon's room Marina asked Leon if he wanted to have sex with her. She was beautiful, sexy and screwed up and Leon knew enough to be wary. Perhaps this was the only way Marina was able to relate to men. It gave her back the power she had lost by exposing her vulnerabilities. He was disappointed in her reversion to type. He had thought their day together was not a prelude to sex but to a deeper connection. But he saw she had a deep need for contact too so mustering all his strength of character, because of course he desired her, he suggested they just share the bed as companions. And to his surprise this is what they did .
Marina slept deeply whereas he had a struggle to control his desire but his time in the monastery helped with that and he understood he was part of a healing process for her.

Next day Leon said goodbye to his landlord of six weeks and the two of them set off. When they arrived in the chaos of Old Delhi Marina kept close to Leon and he led the way to find her a taxi. On the train they had talked a bit about her plans, she had said she thought perhaps she would go back to Art School, maybe in Paris . She had also decided to take his advice and stay a couple of nights in a good hotel in Delhi to recuperate a bit more, to be soothed by the western comfort such hotels provide. The last Leon saw of her was her giving a slight wave from the taxi window .

Thoughtfully Leon shouldered his rucksac and went to find a cheap room. Once settled he opened his bag and tucked into the side pocket was a rolled up drawing. It was of him, sitting under a tree at Sanarth, meditating. It was a lovely drawing, delicate, lightly sketched but it seemed to contain the peace of the holy place . He studied it for a long time . In very small letters at the bottom it said Thank you.

Chapter 11:: Sarah and Jane 1979

Sarah double checked the red strip on the pregnancy test. God, this was a shock, she was in a very casual relationship, if you could even call it that, with another member of the Housing Co_Op where she lived, near Hornsey Art School, scene of the riotous sit-in of 1968. Her career was taking off, she loved what she did, how could she even contemplate having a baby? She had worked hard to get to where she was and felt she was making a difference

She had spent four long years after Uni training to be a solicitor, first working for years in restaurants and bars whilst studying part time for the Legal Practice Qualification and then the required two years work experience before she could practise. She had done this partly in Davy's dads firm, Davy had been doing a PHD at LSE and they saw each other for mad nights every now and then and when an opportunity arose she had jumped at the chance of working for that left wing firm. Her second placement had been with the National Council For Civil Liberties ,Patricia Hewitt had just become the Director and the NCCL was fighting numerous cases for Women, Gay rights and various miscarriages of justice. Sarah´s time there reinforced and developed her feminist commitment , the myriad injustices that women faced fueled her energy. She did work for Womens´ Aid, the newly formed organisation giving refuge to battered women, took on large firms that were doing everything they could to creep through loopholes in the 1975 Equal Pay Act, had fully supported the Grunwick Strike by women to be allowed to join a Union. The seventies was an exciting time for women, new groups and campaigns sprouted like weeds .Sheila Rowbotham's 1973 book ´Women's Consciousness Man's World´ convinced Sarah once and for all that the left would not prioritise women's inequality, the sexual politics of many socialist men were deplorable, women needed their own movement. In the five years since qualifying she was getting known as a passionate and competent campaigner for women and the thought of giving all that up , taking a step back in her career filled her with dread. What should she do? She thought she was probably eight weeks and knew, if she was going to have a termination it was best before 12 weeks. The work she had done ever since Uni with the Abortion Campaign meant she was fully conversant with the details of the legal abortion act. She had a sudden recollection of what Jane had bravely gone through when they were in their second year and how now she was the devoted mum of three, the youngest had just started nursery, the eldest, aged eight ,born when she was 22, soon after University and marriage to Howard. Of course, she decided, she would go and see Jane and discuss her dilemma. She was thirty, maybe she should have this baby she thought. She loved Jane's kids though did not see them often. Jane seemed happy and was a brilliant mother and always made frantically busy Sarah welcome ,and listened with interest and support to her tales of work and campaigns. Sometimes Jane went with Sarah to meetings, though Howard disapproved and had little time for feminism. She made motherhood seem effortless but of course she did not work and there was no way Sarah would give up her career. Having decided that Jane's advice was what she needed, she dressed, rang Jane to fix a date and then went to the office putting the problem behind her.

Ringing Jane's bell, two mornings later, she marshalled her thoughts. Although she and Jane had not seen a great deal of each in the last few years, having taken completely different paths, they were still close, kept in regular contact, still laughed at the same things and shared similar views, though only Sarah put them into practice. Jane managed her family and Howard brilliantly but her world was narrow compared to Sarah's.

"Come in, come in" said Jane "lovely to see you but unexpected, especially on a working day. Is something wrong?"

They hugged each other and Sarah blurted out her news.

"I'm pregnant and don't know what to do"

Jane quickly made coffee and they settled themselves on the sofa in the kitchen. Sarah looked around at the familiar family clutter and as always felt comfortable and at home.

"So what does the father say?" said Jane, getting straight to the point.

"Oh I haven't told him yet, its Jeff, you know him, in the house, but we are not really a couple, just casual and anyway it's my body and my choice"

"And what do you want?"

Sarah felt herself welling up,

"Oh I don't know, I think I want it, once I saw the result my first thought was yes, yes, but then my work, everything I do is so important to me, I'm not you Jane, I just could not stay at home when there is so much to be done. It is not such a stigma anymore to be a single mum but not easy, I have a couple of friends trying to bring up kids on their own."

Sarah started to cry in earnest. Jane had rarely seen tough resilient Sarah cry. She moved closer to her on the sofa and put her arms round her.

Jane made comforting noises and let Sarah talk. Blowing her nose and shaking her tangled curls Sarah said how since 95% of women had children she felt she would understand issues for women better if she had to deal with them herself. How one big divide in the Women's Movement was between those who had children and those who did not.

"Dear Sarah" said Jane "only you would have a political reason for having a baby!"

Sarah laughed ruefully,

"The big issue is how do I keep on working.? I love what I do and am making a difference I know. And how would I manage with a baby living in the Co_OP.? Its a bit chaotic there as you know, I don't know how a baby would fit in"

Six of them shared the big old house and only three of them had proper jobs, a teacher, Sarah and a charity worker. The other 3 picked up casual work and were creatives. Sarah sighed deeply

"O it's impossible"

"What will your parents say?" asked Jane

"Oh I think they would point out all the difficulties but would support me whatever I did.". Brightening she said

"You know they have always disapproved of me living in the housing co-op, have several times offered to lend me a deposit to buy my own place. I could do that..have a spare room for a lodger to help..and to babysit!!

"Darling, sounds like you want this baby but not sure how you will cope" summarised Jane

Sarah let out a sigh, already it was clearer to her that she did want to go ahead with the pregnancy but was deeply worried about the logistics. Maternity leave depended on the employer and Sarah´s firm of Solicitors, since it took on mainly legal aid work, was not very well off, the State covered 6 weeks and then no more money came in.

Jane and she spent the rest of the morning discussing how Sarah would manage . She could try and negotiate going back to work part time for a while, so would only need a childminder for half the week. Some employers sacked you if you were pregnant but she was sure that would not be true of her progressive firm. When they were on their third cup of coffee Jane said

"Molly has just started nursery you know and for the first time in 8 years I am free. I have been vaguely thinking about doing some further study, An MA maybe in literature."

"oh Jane that's brilliant" interrupted Sarah, who had always thought Jane was wasting her brains in domesticity.

" But perhaps I could look after the baby, it is only half the week after all and I miss having a baby at home?"

Sarah stared at her old friend,
"My God, would you really do that? that would be wonderful, perfect," she started to cry "oh I am so emotional these days, not like me at all"

"That's all the crazy hormones kicking in" said Jane "but really I would love to do that"

"What would Howard say? And I would pay you of course"

"Leave Howard to me, I will tell him it's a part time job, which it will be but one I love and don't worry about money, Howard earns far more than we need.""

They hugged passionately, these two old friends, as always helping and supporting each other.

Baby Mary (after Wollstonecraft) was born on 1st of May, and three days later Margaret Thatcher was elected Prime Minister. Sarah´s life and that of Britain was about to change irrevocably.

The 1980s were a frantic time for Sarah and for all those who opposed the draconian changes Thatcher made to the very fabric of Britain. The breakdown of the post war consensus, the privatisation of the nationalised industries, the shift from community to individuality, the notion there was no such thing as society, only families looking out for themselves, all corrupted and distorted the very nature of the country. She returned to work full time when Mary was 2, having found a full time childminder. Jane, in 1981 started an MA Birkbeck college , she shone at her studies, was writing lots of poetry. Howard had only supported her studying if she went part time so she was usually home for the children. However full or part time it was still a juggling act to fit everything in and she had the double burden of trying to make it seem as if nothing was different at home now that she was working. It was this that made Jane fully understand the arguments of the Women's´ Movement.

Life was more complicated for Sarah but Jane was still always there as a back up when her complicated arrangements broke down. Fortunately Carol, the childminder, lived near Jane so if Sarah was delayed at work she was there to pick up Mary. Sarah was busy, her firm fighting attempts to abolish child benefits, of changes in the immigration act, of examples of increasing reduction in civil rights. Jane too was becoming radicalised, partly through discussions with younger students at college and partly through her lived experience. The establishment of a base for American Cruise Nuclear missiles at Greenham Common was what changed Jane from a sympathetic ear to Sarah's impassioned arguments to a campaigner.

Jane s only youthful foray into politics when she was at school had been to support the Campaign for Nuclear Disarmament, she wore the badge on her school uniform, her family church supported CND and even her parents thought it alright to go to the meetings, indeed one of her fathers colleagues was a supporter.

The cold war between America and Russia was hotting up. The Government had issued all households with a pamphlet *Protect and Survive* about what to do if there was a nuclear attack. Prepare a cupboard under the stairs! Stockpile tinned food! Expect to survive! People were anxious. Then Sarah gave her a pamphlet by the radical historian EP Thomson, *Protest and Survive* and she understood acceptance was not the answer. The government had given the Americans permission to station their nuclear missiles on British Soil. On Greenham Common, idyllic common land near Newbury.

By now Jane had joined a local Women's Group, all professional women like herself with a keen interest in the politics which affected women. They read and discussed *Protest and Survive* and when the women who had set up a peace camp at Greenham called for a day of action they all decided to go, with their children. Jane braced herself to tell Howard her plans :

" You know the mothers group, Howard?" She began the week before the planned action. She never referred to her Womens group as that, she had long since decided that mothers was less threatening to Howard than women.

"hmm, What ?"
 he said, shaking the Financial Times. They were at the breakfast table, a Saturday morning. The children had dispersed, the boys playing with their lego in the sitting room and Molly watching television, her Saturday morning treat.

" Well, next weekend we have decided to go to Greenham Common for a rally against the nuclear weapons stationed there, it's a family day out for women and children"

" What ? Sounds a funny sort of family day out"

"Well , it is against the Cruise missiles being there and will be peaceful and fun for the children"

"How will it be fun? A bunch of lesbians and scruffy campaigners causing trouble. I don't like the sound of it"

"Oh Howard, its women, there won't be trouble and you agree with me it is dangerous to have American weapons on British soil"

"Hmph" Howard had glanced at *Protest and Survive* when Jane was talking about it, she had been very upset at the implications for the family and for the future and he had gone along with her arguments. Howard believed in anything for a quiet life and, until she started her course, that's what Jane had given him. However he had learnt early on that his seemingly docile and pliable Jane had a core of determination . The bewildered and battered girl he had married had matured into a grounded and thoughtful woman, sometimes he felt uneasy with how she was changing, but daily life ran as smoothly as ever, the children were happy and Jane was spreading her wings . Only natural, he thought.
" And it's not lesbians and what you said, that's really awful to say that, its mothers like me, from all over and our group can hardly be described as scruffy !"

" Yes well, I suppose it's ok…"

" Good, well we are going so I am glad you agreed"

Later , when he went for a round of golf with his friend Charley, whose wife Helen was a friend of Jane's and another mother at the school, he checked with him.

"O just some nonsense" said Charley . " They think they can make a difference but they will soon find out, no bad thing to let them see first hand how pointless it is"

Helen had organised a mini bus to take them all to Greenham, 6 mothers and 12 children piled in and set off from North London. They had balloons to tie on the base, artificial flowers, scarves. Some of the children had brought soft toys to decorate the fence. This was something different, a womens' protest, a peaceful protest, a protest for a safe future for their families. As they drew nearer to Newbury they saw more and more coaches arriving.

" o Sarah, this reminds me of when we went on the Grosvenor square demo in 68, all the coaches " said Jane .

" I know, same energy but this will be different, you'll see, no men, no aggro"

" Paul got hurt didn't he, and Davey spent the night in the cells. Oh and the poor horses, I was so shocked at the police charging us."

" And that was America again, our government blindly supporting them"

They arrived and piled out of the bus, Helen went off to find a parking spot. They agreed to wait for her by the Blue gate . The women at the camp had named each of the gates and each gate had a camp, with tents and makeshift benders. The children were all fascinated, there was so much to look at. Some women were dressed up in crazy costumes, others sported banners, flags, more balloons. More and more women were arriving, Helen reappeared and they all set off to find a section of fence to embrace, the plan was to completely encircle the base. They passed embroidered banners threaded through the wire, a huge white flower fixed up high .

" Look Jane, that's made of tampons and sanitary towels!" laughed Sarah.

" This is wonderful, it's all so creative and life affirming." Said Jane.

"Here's a stretch for us" said Helen

They helped the children tie on their toys, blew up balloons, threaded scarves and ribbons through the wire.

Thirty thousand women came that December day to Greenham. Children walking ,in slings ,in pushchairs ,on their mothers backs. All embraced the base.
They sang " We shall not, we shall not be moved" they laughed , they kissed, they wept " The Earth is our Mother she will take care of us" they sang. The moment was one of power, of solidarity, of hope. A huge army of women, the repercussions were world wide,

nothing had been seen like it before, the years of campaigning with men were over, this was a womens´ action .

They finally left, arrived back in London and Helen dropped Sarah and Jane and the children at Jane's house.

"How did you get on ?"asked Howard "how are the children?"

" Daddy Daddy" they all talked at once , overlapping in their excitement. .

"We saw puppets"

There were lots of balloons"

"We saw soldiers with guns"

"We sang and danced" "

"There was millions and millions of mummies"

Jane and Sarah exchanged a glance

"I told you Howard, it would be a fun day out for the children" said Jane

Chapter 12 : Maerdy,South Wales, 1984

Sarah straightened up and rubbed the small of her aching back. She was tired, had been up at six to meet Doug and the van at seven..

Daughter Mary had stayed the night at Jane's so she could make an early start. Apart from a brief stop for a coffee just before the Severn bridge they had powered down from London making good time. So far, she had unloaded eight boxes of food, carrying them into the hall for the local women to unpack and organise on long trestle tables. The Miners' Institute would be open from eleven for villagers to come and get much needed supplies, it was a military operation, the turn around had to be quick because from twelve the Miners Wives would be serving lunch. For most, in this the eighth month of the strike, their only hot meal of the day. People were tightening their belts, money was short but resolve was long. Autumn was drawing in ,families were worried about keeping warm, lads were scavenging in the slag heaps that littered the valley, searching for burnable coal. As the numbers of police increased, up to sixty thousand now protecting the tiny percentage of miners who were still working, the strikers and their supporters became more and more convinced that this was a battle with the Government, not the Coal Board. The more pressure by the police, the more scenes of violence, baton charges and horses galloping at pickets the more justifiably angry the miners became.

  Support of the struggle was widespread. Early on in the strike Sarah's local Labour party had got a list of towns and villages needing support. She had a jolt of memory when she saw Maerdy on the list, surely that was where Paul came from, she remembered them all going down for his funeral. She decided, though her work commitments were heavy, to sign up . She had been coming for six months now, usually twice a month. People were generous, understanding that the strikers had no money coming in and families to feed.

Looking around, her eyes wandering to the slag heaps that overlooked the village and above to a grey sky, she thought of the first time she'd come down with the Crouch End Labour group. There had been four of them that day, now it was usually just her and Doug. Others loaded up the night before and helped sort and box the steady supply of donations. That first time, driving up the Rhonda Valley once past Newport they had all fallen silent as they travelled through pit villages, rows and rows of dark terraced houses, two up and two down opening onto the pavement. A flash of memory had come to Sarah, of going to Paul's parents house after the funeral, all crammed into the neat and polished front room, the best room, rarely used and afterwards going upstairs to see Paul's old bedroom. She had resolved on that first trip to try and make contact with his parents.

Once they arrived and after the first flurries of welcome and unloading she asked around for a Mrs. Evans, Paul's mother, but quickly realised that in South Wales she needed to be more specific. She confided to a particularly chatty woman that she had been a friend of this Mrs Evans' son at University.

"O lass you must be one of those English that came to his funeral. Yes, she's in the hall, come with me" said the woman.

She bustled ahead and Sarah, following in her wake, saw a small woman with dyed black hair and a bright scarf setting out cups by a tea urn.

"Look you Megan, look who's here, one of your Paul's old friends"
The woman looked up startled, and after a minute she said:
" Why Yes, I remember you"
"I'm Sarah, I was in the band with him"
"Yes of course, and you came to the house, o you were a bonny girl, you had a black lace dress., who would have thought…"

Instinctively Sarah embraced her, an embrace that was warmly returned.
" I often think of Paul, so when I saw my Labour Party branch had Maerdy on their list, well I just had to come here and help, for his sake"
"Well bless you .We need all the help we can get. It's been a tough old time but this all helps".
Her eyes watered, but after a strong sniff she said:
"So when you've finished unloading, maybe we can sit down together, have a good chat. Paul's dad will want to see you but not today, he's off to Yorkshire on the picket line'
"Don't worry, I will come as often as I can and we can catch up properly." said Sarah.
So that was the beginning of a deepening relationship between Sarah, Megan and the feisty miner's wives. Once it was known she was a lawyer people started asking her for all kinds of advice. Her firm was handling various cases brought by the NUM against the police, Sarah was well informed and filled with righteous anger at

the brutality that was daily reported on in the left wing press. Her visits developed into a routine, she would unload, then sit by Megan at the tea urn chatting to people and putting them in touch with organisations and charities that were helping the strike and advising on everything from legal aid to contraception. Each visit she came to admire the miners' wives more. They were hugely well organised, making a hot lunch out of virtually nothing for the miners everyday, some were joining the flying pickets, going with their men in coaches to picket the mines that were still open. Sarah saw the strength and confidence of these women grow, their total support for the struggle. Many loved to chat with her, ask her about what she did in London, scoffed but listened when she broadened the talk to feminism and her involvement with the women's movement .

" Ee lass, he gives me my wages on a Friday , I give him back some beer money and then I am in charge' one woman said to her when they were discussing power. They understood the power of the bosses, the power of the union but womens´ powerlessness did not seem to have any meaning for these tough working class women.She was struck by the woman referring to her wages , knew if she mentioned the Wages for Housework group they would laugh with derision but she wondered actually how much common ground there was.

She shook herself, came back to the present and decided to unload two more boxes then take a break. Doug could finish off. Some women were already arriving early with their shopping bags to check out the fresh vegetables ,toiletries, tins, rice, pasta, teabags ,coffee, a life line. Each time Sarah was impressed by the sense of community and determination of the women. They laughed and joked at some of the produce laid out, the toiletries from well meaning Londoners caused particular derision, especially the range for men that had found their way on to the table.

"What's these for?" asked one woman, holding up a tin of anchovies.

"Couldn't make much of a meal from that little tin" responded another

"Salty fish, can have it on pizza" Megan chipped in.

Sarah put down her last two boxes which Megan started unloading "Oo all fresh veg here" she said..

"we´ll have this lot for the kitchen, can make a good veggie stew for tomorrow."

Sarah went to the urn and poured herself a cup of tea

"I'll be back in a minute, just going to have a ciggy outside" she said to Megan.

Taking a pull on her cigarette she moved to stand opposite the hall on a patch of grass, and then her attention was caught by a flurry of activity , several men and one woman were standing in a huddle, beside a large BBC van , a camera and boom microphone were in evidence held by one of the men. At the centre of the small group was a tall distinctive figure, with thick brown hair and a purposeful air, a stab of recognition went through her, surely that was Gideon? Sarah was aware of his success, that he worked for the BBC, had seen his name on several hard-hitting documentaries. Stubbing out her cigarette she hurried over to the group.

"Gideon?' she said.

He turned irritably, looked at her blankly:

"It's Sarah, from Brighton, the Ranters?" she said embarrassed but holding her ground.

With dawning recognition, he said, with a laugh :

'Wow ,Sarah, yes of course. Hi, how are you? what are you doing here?"

"A food run from London, miners support group" she said 'And you?"

" oh, we are filming, going to all the striking pit villages, putting together a documentary on how they are holding out , groups like yours are part of the story. We filmed one in Treforest earlier on today"

" You do realise this is where Paul was from? Paul? Our drummer? That's why I came. Actually maybe the last time I saw you was at his funeral, here, must be 16 years ago"

An unreadable look crossed Gideon's face. Sarah wondered later if he had even realised where he was.

" Ah yes" he said "Yes," and he looked around as if seeking confirmation.

" Actually, Ivé got friendly with his mum, she helps in the hall every week, why don't you come and say hello, she would love that. She asks after you, after all of us"

Gideon looked back at the camera man and others, waiting by the

van, the camera was now disassembled. He hesitated and then said " Ah, no time, sorry, we're on a tight schedule, some of this stuff is for tonight's news, got to get on. Give her my best regards, say I said Hello and sorry I couldn't stop. Amazing to see you, take care, bye"
" Just five minutes? She would be so pleased"
Turning away, over his shoulder he said " Not on, can't be done. Bye." he walked over to the BBC van. Sarah stood stock still looking after him . Was that it? A dismissal? Yes, this callousness, this self-absorption was just how he'd been with Jane. Surely he could have spared five minutes?Thinking back to Paul's funeral she remembered his touching eulogy, he seemed to show sweetness then and empathy. It seemed that tenderness ,fleeting as it was ,was now completely overlaid by his ambition. Resolving not to mention this encounter to Megan she went back into the hall, ruminating that once a shit always a shit .

On the long drive back to London she was mainly silent, thinking over the exchanges with Gideon, thinking yet again about the year they had lived together, the band, Paul. And Gideon the elusive centre of it all.

' Penny for them" said Doug, after many miles had passed

' Did you notice that BBC van in the village, up from the hall? Said Sarah

" Yeh, what was that about ?"

" So, I recognised the guy in charge, Gideon March, I was at Uni with him, and Paul, you know Megan's son who died? We were all in a band together"

" Yes, of course, you told me. I've heard of him, didn't he make that documentary series about housing and homelessness a couple of years ago?'

"Yeh. Well I went over to talk to him, I thought he might come and say hello to Megan. He made a speech at Paul's funeral. Paul hero worshipped him..." Sarah fell silent

" And ?" said Doug.

" He said he had no time, had to go and to give her his best regards"
Doug said nothing for a bit and then, glancing at Sarah, he said

" Well, he sounds a right arsehole"

Laughing weakly, she replied

" yeh, well he always was"

For the rest of the journey they chatted about the miners' solidarity march that was coming up and other things. They had to return the van and meet up with some of the others in the group. She did not have to pick up Mary until Sunday morning, Jane was taking all the children to the Natural History museum, a favourite haunt of her boys, and 5 year old Mary and 8 year old Molly loved charging around the long galleries . Jane laughingly protested whenever Sarah apologetically asked yet again for her to look after Mary because of work and campaigning demands. .

"We love it, the girls love being together and it's my contribution to the feminist cause, I'm Martha to your Mary love."

Sarah wondered whether to tell Jane about seeing Gideon but, just as she had decided not to tell Megan she decided no point in telling Jane . Very occasionally they spoke of Gideon, when his name was in the news or they had both seen one of his programmes. Sarah sensed Jane was uncomfortable revisiting those days in St Agnes avenue and her agonising relationship with Gideon. Best to leave alone, thought Sarah, both of them had come a long way since then.

Chapter 13 : 2017

" Alright Janey ?" asked Howard, glancing over at his wife and shaking out his paper. They were having breakfast in their sunny conservatory. It was early June, the garden was full of flowers, the sound of cars a distant hum .
" Hmmm, sorry,yes," Jane shook her head, she had been miles away,
"I was just thinking whether this weekend in Suffolk is such a good idea"
" Oh come on, it will be fun, finally everyones agreed a date, we can all reminisce , remember Gideon, get drunk, relive our youth a bit"
as Howard burbled on Jane thought, not for the first time, how her husband seemed to live in a different world from her. Did he not remember how awful, how agonising, how shameful those long ago days had been? But then of course they had also been glorious, wild and wonderful, at least at first. She had gone back after her

breakdown and did the third year, getting a First, but still damaged and depressed, she had married Howard who had been a loyal presence all along. Three babies had followed this early marriage in quick succession and Jane had settled for a life of safe domesticity.

"Oh well, I expect your right"
Satisfied Howard returned to the financial pages of his paper and Jane picked up the culture section.
It had taken several emails to get a date they could all manage. Dates had to be arranged around Davy's visits from France. Leon had offered only three possible weekends, Jane wondered if he regretted his impulsive offer at Gideon's funeral. Sarah, bless her, had been flexible so in the end a date at the end of June fell into place. She wondered if it would be intrusive to suggest they all brought their own bedding and then told herself just because Leon lived alone it did not mean he did not have spare sheets.

The truth was, as she acknowledged to herself, she was nervous, nervous of spending time with Leon and resuscitating things better left buried. Leon had been so thoughtful and kind to her when she was ill. Even now she could hardly bear to name the utter total despair she had fallen into after Paul's death and Gideon's casual cruelty. She supposed it was a breakdown, well of course it was, and Leon had sat with her, Leon had found her, half conscious after drinking half a bottle of whisky and taking handfuls of aspirin. He had made her sick, walked her all night up and down her tumbled room. She could never forget that he had saved her, only now, all these years later did she wonder how he had felt about it all and why it was he was there. The awful self obsession of youth, she was so wrapped up and tortured by her own feelings she had no room to try and decipher the misery on his face.

A year after the events of that summer Leon had gone to India, had joined the hippy trail , she had had cryptic cards from him, once a long, stained air mail letter from Dharamsala which she could make no sense of. Seeing him at Gideons funeral had been a shock, the same quiet presence, the same Leon.

Clearing the breakfast things after Howard had left, Jane thought perhaps she would phone Sarah. They had spoken the day after Gideon's funeral, Sarah had said she had barely slept that night, her mind endlessly replaying scenes from the past.
"Maybe a weekend in Suffolk will lay some ghosts" she had said.

Although she and Sarah had been so close back then, had had such fun together, Jane knew there had been secrets. She was always aware that Sarah was infuriated by Gideon and was irritated although she tried to disguise it with Jane's increasing enthralment. She thought back to when they had first met Gideon, it was late spring , Sarah's 19th birthday and they had got drunk, two young women, not used to alcohol.

She stood, irresolutely ,by the french doors. Should she get on with the garden? Go up to her study and finish off her marking? Or phone Sarah? She went upstairs, pausing to look out of the landing window at the garden, no, she told herself, I'll phone Sarah and then I'll get on with my day. As she dialled the familiar number she wondered if Leon had a garden. She listened to the phone ringing, nearly hung up and then:

"Hello 634291" she could hear children's shrill voices in the background

"Sarah ,it's Jane. Sorry have you got the children?'

" Yes, but it's fine,they're painting, God help me,as long as they're making a mess they are happy" laughed Sarah.

Twins Chloe and Ben were six and the light of Sarah's life. When Mary, her daughter, was young she had spent almost as much time with Jane and her three as she had with her mum. Sarah had been so busy with her career and women's politics , was always rushing from one meeting to another that she had missed many of the milestones of childhood and adolescence. School concerts, sports days, , it was Jane who guided Mary through her first period, it having happened when Sarah was at a conference. Sarah´s maternal position was one of permanent guilt. It was a total revelation to her when she moved to Bristol to be near Mary and the children how much she enjoyed them. She had endless patience with the twins, loved their crazy company and being silly with them. She was a completely different person from the ambitious and often angry feminist of her working years. ..no pressure, no pull to what she ought to be doing. She confided in Jane she'd been too preoccupied to be a mother, she had found motherhood got in the way, was frustrating and boring , but now she felt she had been given a second chance, found grand-motherhood fascinating and an utter joy.

"Thank goodness" she had added " Mary bears no grudges and is just glad to have my help"

" How's things Jane?" she continued.

" Fine, but actually I have been worrying about the coming weekend. It seems strange to be going to stay with someone we haven't seen for 40 years. It might be, well, really awful, awkward. Oh ,I don't know.." she tailed off.

"O.k.' said Sarah briskly. "It could be, but we three are friends, we've seen Davey occasionally and anyway he's always entertaining company. Remember at the funeral?"

" Yes," said Jane hesitantly.

" I suppose it's Leon. He was always so, so enigmatic . But I keep remembering how kind he was to me when all that stuff happened. You weren't there, but he was so kind to me. And then, after I came back I hardly saw him again"

" Jane" Sarah was firm. "We may or may not go over all that but if we do, surely it will be for the good?" Her voice changed from soft concern for her friend to stern adult

" Oh Ben you naughty boy"

" Sorry darling, better go, Ben's tipped his water over Chloe's painting."

Jane could hear howls in the background.

"It will be alright, I'll be there, you'll see we'll have a good time.

See you Friday . Love" and she hung up.

Jane sighed, Sarah was and had always been a support, ever since they met on their first day at Uni Sarah had egged her on, encouraged and sustained her. Over the years sometimes the roles had been reversed, especially when Mary had been a difficult teenager but Jane knew, with Sarah there, nothing awful could happen in Suffolk. Not for the first time she mused how she was much closer to Sarah than she was to Howard even if months could go by without them seeing each other.

She thought about the big old house she and Sarah had moved into in their second year. There were 6 of them and Miss Pink the sitting tenant on the top floor. Gideon and Paul, both dead, Marina who knew where, and now, the survivors, Sarah, Leon and Davey were to meet up. Howard had never lived in the house, just as he had never been in the band.

She thought "I'll be positive. Maybe I'll see if I can find any old photos from then to take with me "

She shook herself, went back down stairs and got her gardening gloves and a trowel from by the back door. She decided she would put in a good hour or so on the big border and finish her marking after lunch. And who knows, she mused, perhaps Sarah was right and the weekend in Suffolk would be for the good.

Chapter 14 Suffolk

Leon was hoeing the onion bed and wondering, not for the first time, why on earth he had invited his old university crowd to stay for the weekend. It was an odd set of coincidences which had led him to Gideon's funeral back in April. When he had got Claire's collective email he had made a note of the time and place, but not with any intention of going. He had only been back in England a year, had had no interest really in renewing old contacts, looking up old friends. Shortly afterwards, unpacking the last of the boxes which had been left in his mother's house and had moved with him to Suffolk, he had found a letter from Gideon, dated 1969 and various other fliers and mementos of that turbulent time. Then a meeting he had to go to in London was fixed for the day before the funeral and it seemed somehow inevitable that he should make the effort to attend. But that did not explain his offer of having them all to stay, made at the reception afterwards. Perhaps, he wondered, surprising himself, it was Jane's discomfited blush when he had mentioned her poetry.

He remembered how, when they all lived together and apart in St.Agnes Avenue, going into the communal kitchen where Jane sat alone, writing at the table . It was the first time since they had all moved in that he had talked to her on her own. She wore her dark hair long in those days, long and straight with a shine when she was happy and, he came to notice, lank and dull when, as became increasingly frequent, she was distressed. They talked about poetry and she shyly offered the poem she was working on. After that conversation she occasionally used to leave a folder of poems on the chair just inside the door of his room. Sometimes he would scribble a changed word or a comment but mainly nothing, just Thank you.

When he had finished the onions, he noted with satisfaction there were plenty of peas that needed picking and checking the raspberry canes, though there would probably be enough raspberries for dinner. Maybe some of the others would pick? There was no time now, he better wash and check the rooms he had got ready. He had had to buy new bed linen, did not have enough for three bedrooms, towels as well. His was a solitary life, he had had no previous guests. He thought that his friendship with Gideon, 40 years ago, had probably been the most intense he had ever had.

Theirs was an odd friendship; their backgrounds totally different, their personalities, one extrovert, one introvert, opposites in every way but they shared a common passion for music, both loved playing and were into the same obscure bands. Their differences stimulated them, they tested themselves against each other. Leon found Gideon infuriating and Gideon no doubt found Leon detached . They had ferocious arguments about politics, about art, about books, about how to cook spaghetti bolognaise, how best to roll a joint, about anything and everything. Both were, by nature, argumentative and didactic, sharp, quick witted, both were in the process of reinventing and discovering themselves.

Leon went back downstairs. It was nearly five pm and Jane had said she and Howard would drive up from London, arriving between five and six.

Leon wondered how much she thought about those times. It was she, he thought, who had proposed this weekend when they all met at the funeral, or was it Sarah? It was because of the events of that summer of 69 that his life had gone the way it had. He also suspected that Jane had married steady, faithful, unimaginative Howard because of what had happened back then.

They had all lived together in the big old house, with Miss Pink quietly on the top floor, for a year and then Paul had died, Jane had her breakdown, Marina disappeared and everything flew apart, like pieces in a kaleidoscope. He, Gideon and Howard had somehow managed to take their Finals, God knows how, the resilience of youth he supposed. All of that had happened that June and it was June now some 40 years on

Of course Sarah and Jane had gone back to university for their final year and so, surprisingly, had Davy who had somehow got accepted on an MA course. The girls still lived together but no longer at St. Agnes Avenue. Davy, he remembered, had moved into Marina's old room at the Trip Out Café on the seafront.

He had gone back home to Sheffield, desperate to get as far away as possible, he worked long hours in menial jobs and in a year had saved enough to go travelling. He wrote Jane occasional letters and she sent him poems ,she was writing like one possessed ,which perhaps she was. A couple of times he went down to Brighton to see Davy and Jane and Sarah. Jane was focusing on her work but some of her old spark was resurfacing. There was news of Gideon, he had come back from California, had got a graduate traineeship at the BBC. Davy saw him in London when he went home. Gideon no longer knew the whereabouts of Marina, he had left her in California and apparently did not want to talk about her .

Once he had saved enough money he went off to India, his fascination with the Brighton Pavilion made that choice inevitable. He was away for three years, travelling through Iran, Iraq, and Afghanistan. He earned bits of money teaching English and when he finally came back to England he took a TEFL course, later he added a PHD. in linguistics and began a career with the British Council that had lasted 30 years.

He felt emotionally drained; it was a long time since he had thought about those student days and this reunion weekend had not even begun. Someone would have to pick Davy and Sarah up from the station; their trains arrived conveniently close together. Then they would have dinner. He could think no further than that. A car sounded its horn, a BMW came to a tidy halt by the sheds and Jane got out of the passenger door, her hair glossy and her neat figure clothed in a pale blue sundress,

"Here we are," she said. The weekend had begun.

Davy had put in a productive day's work at the British Library, was running late but just managed to catch the train at Liverpool Street, bound for Suffolk. He bought a bottle of wine at the buffet and settled back in his seat in the first Class. He felt he deserved the treat, both wine and comfort, as work was going well, in fact he had made a bit of a breakthrough. His mobile rang, it was Janine, ringing from France.

"Hello love, yes, I'm on the train. just made it in time, work went really well today,"

He and Janine, his French wife, had finally settled permanently in France three years before, when Davy had taken the suggested early retirement from the university. They had had a home there for years, near Janine's parents in rural Brittany. Davy did not want to make the move, arguing he needed to be near libraries and London. The compromise was his small flat and he came over as often as he felt he could get away with. Janine was a painter, used to being on her own, she was pragmatic and knew her wicked Davy needed the bright lights but she stipulated he must spend a minimum of 60% of his time in France. She was a very good cook, as his incipient paunch testified and since he had cut down dramatically on his drinking and no longer smoked, the pleasures of the table figured high on Davy's requirements for a good life. When in London he found it all too easy to fall back into his old habits, after a stint in the British Library if given half the chance he would frequent afternoon drinking clubs or the pubs around Soho. He knew it was a good thing, he now spent a lot of his time in Brittany but was finding it difficult to settle into the next stage of his life. He was still asked to sit on panels, to speak at Festivals, had articles commissioned. The word was out that he had pulled himself together, was more reliable and was less likely to embarrass himself and others with his bad behaviour. As with most semi reformed reprobates Davy had a fondness for his days of excess, the ghastly times obliterated along with brain cells and only the warm camaraderie of drunken nights remained.

    He sighed with satisfaction, the wine went down well. He was looking forward to the weekend, could not remember who had suggested it but thought it might have been Sarah. He sipped reflectively on his drink.

He and she had had a bit of a thing he remembered when they all lived together in St. Agnes Avenue.

The so-called quiet carriage was noisy with crying children. It was a Friday and the train was crowded. Fortunately Sarah had reserved a seat but her neighbour was a fat and sweaty young man who had so far eaten two bags of crisps, a packet of sandwiches and drunk a can of beer, and they were not long out of Liverpool Street. She closed her eyes and resigned herself to an uncomfortable journey. It would be fun to spend time with Davy again, she mused, she and he had slept together on a fairly regular basis that 2nd year. She remembered talking to Jane about him., laughing about free love and lack of possessiveness. It all seemed so long ago, in a time before she had become committed to feminist politics, that free love benefited the boys more than the girls. No one cool wanted to be thought uptight. Jane, sweet innocent Jane as she had been then, before everything happened, found it hard not to dwell on love. It was a period, she thought, when they had all been trying out different selves.

The journey was nearly over, she had been so wrapped in her thoughts she had been unaware of her obnoxious neighbour getting off earlier. The train was slowing down, looking out of the window she saw the name of the station, She had arrived.

She struggled off the train, heaving her wheelie bag down from the carriage and looked around for the station exit. She heard her name called and looking behind her saw an exuberant Davy bounding up the platform.

"Looks like we were on the same train" he said, giving her a bear hug. She felt embarrassed, given the thoughts she had been having on the journey about him and found it hard to reconcile this wine-breathed overweight semi stranger with the Davy of her reminiscence.

"Hmm, but I can't afford first class" she replied somewhat tartly to cover her confusion.
"Well, I thought I deserved it, I've had a good day. Come on, let's ring old Leon and get the party going".
Sarah thought he had started on his own already but then chided herself for being churlish. They went outside and sat on a bench in the afternoon sun to wait for their lift. Sarah lit up and Davy inhaled alongside her.
"Oh, you devil, still smoking?" he said. "My doctor made me quit"
O, I only smoke 2 or 3 a day" she said defensively
"Make sure you let me know when you have one then so I can have

a whiff" he said.

Companionable now, they looked around and exchanged snippets about their lives. Sarah mused, not for the first time, how with some people, even if you have not seen them for years and years you can just fall back into old patterns and rhythms. The half serious half joking relationship that had been theirs fell over them like a comfortable old coat. They were laughing, like the old friends they were as a black BMW drew up in front of their bench.

Howard, for it was he, got out of the car and opening the boot said "Well you two seem to have rolled back the years."

"Hey, Howard, being our roadie again?" said Davy, clapping him on the back.

They stowed their luggage, Davy getting in the front and with a roar they were off.

Leon had intended going to the station to meet Sarah and Davy himself but when their call came Howard had insisted that he would go.

"I´ll be much quicker than you and more room for their luggage than your old banger" he said, having noticed Leon's battered Citroen Diane when he and Jane had arrived. Leon laughed,

"Well if you're sure, Jane and I can pick raspberries and start organising dinner"

After blundering about looking for his jacket and keys and repeating the directions to the station Howard was off and Jane and Leon were left alone. A silence fell between them, they looked at each other and then Leon said

"It's an hour there and back to the station, plenty of time. Come on I´ll show you the garden and my veg patch"

"Lovely" said Jane. "You are very domestic., it's all so nice here" Her gaze took in the terracotta tiled floor, the untidy old welsh dresser jumbled with cups, plates,garden twine, postcards and the detritus of a life. The kitchen table and chairs were mismatched and worn but well used rather than shabby. There was a jug of marigolds on the table and a pile of newspapers. A thin orange cat sidled through the open back door.

"That's Snap" said Leon, as the cat went over to a food bowl by the stove.

"He moved in just after me, no idea where he came from"

"Oh I have two, one of ours just appeared too" laughed Jane "it's what they do"

Leon screwed up his eyes

 "Didn't we have one at the house when we all lived together, and you wrote a funny poem about it crapping everywhere?"said Leon

"Fancy you remembering that" said Jane. " Actually Paul brought it, he found it somewhere. We didn't have it for long, it seemed to make messes in Gideon´s room most and drove Marina wild. It just vanished after a few weeks."

"Yes, well I always thought Marina got rid of it somehow, she was always quite ruthless where her own interests were concerned."
Jane looked at him in surprise, there was a note in his voice which made her want to ask more but she did not know how.

"Come on" he said, taking a bowl off the dresser, "let's pick the raspberries"

The late afternoon sun cast a mellow golden light over the vegetable garden as they navigated their way past spreading courgette plants and tall rows of runner beans. Jane breathed deeply, it was grand to be out of London, late bees droned, birds began their evening song. They began picking the beautiful dark red soft fruit in a gentle quiet. The bowl was filling fast when Jane became aware that Leon had stopped picking and was studying her.

"You haven't changed much Jane. You look very well, very…"he paused. Jane blushed, that wretched blush that had bedevilled her all her life

"Very what?" she asked.

"Oh, sleek, somehow, not forlorn like you used to"

Jane felt tears prick behind her eyes, she reached down to pick some hidden berries and made no answer. Leon, sensing her unease, started to talk of his garden, his late discovery of the pleasures of growing things . Jane was a keen gardener and so, talking of perennials and compost, aphids and weeds they strolled back to the house.

By the time Howard, Davy and Sarah arrived the table was set, potatoes peeled, the casserole which Leon had prepared the day before, in the oven and both were sipping white wine as they picked over the raspberries.

"Well this all looks very cosy and domestic" said Davy, dumping his bag and looking around. Leon stood, and after greetings, embraces and awkward laughter took on his role as host saying

"Right I'll show you your rooms and then I think we should all catch the end of the day outside with a drink"

Sarah and Jane went upstairs together followed by the men and before long they were all assembled outside the back door, sitting around on an assortment of chairs positioned to catch the evening sun. The scent of Lilies wafted over from large pots on the terrace.

"Oh Leon, this is nice" said Sarah "Are you a keen gardener?"

"Well, I was lucky, although the house had been empty for a while there were remnants of a very good garden. I have never had a garden before and I really enjoy the challenge"

"Well Jane and you will have a lot to talk about" said Howard. "Its her passion, I sometimes think she cares more for her plants than me" he guffawed

Sarah slightly raised an eyebrow at Jane who gave a small smile

"Well, plants are more manageable than you, darling" she said lightly.

"Janine grows vegetables." Offered Davy and, talking of the new vogue for vegetable growing, the respective merits of organic or judicious use of Roundup the time passed. The light was fading, the bottle of wine was finished so gathering themselves up they went into the warmly lit kitchen, exclaiming over the delicious smell of the casserole.

Their first evening together passed pleasantly. There was a lot to cover, 40 years and more, lots of gaps in their knowledge of each other. Howard spoke of his job in the city, Jane of their three children now all grown and the delights of grandchildren. Sarah talked about her decision to give up campaigning and to move to Bristol. Davy told funny stories of his career as a pundit on television, his academic work and his recent domicile in France. He too had children from two previous marriages and made passing mention of them. Leon's life was the most unknown, after all both Davy and Sarah had had some public recognition and Jane and Sarah and kept in touch all their lives. They asked him about the different countries he had worked in, Davy especially interested in his Balkan years. The talk ebbed and flowed, another bottle of wine was opened, stories of their lives since their student days were swapped but only glancing reference was made by anyone to their shared days in ST. Agnes Avenue.

Howard was the first to flag, they had moved from the kitchen to Leon's sitting room, fatally Howard had the most comfortable chair. When for the third time a loud snore came from his corner Jane said

"Howard, Howard dear, wake up "

"Humph, Dropped off did I? Think I'll go on up.."

After Howard had gone the four of them looked at each other.

"Shall we have a night cap then?" said Davy and he produced a bottle of Glen Livet from his bag. Sarah and Leon both said yes but Jane went into the kitchen and made herself a cup of tea. Once they were all settled with their drinks Sarah looked around and said:

"Well, I am glad we are here, it's great to see everybody, thank you so much Leon for your hospitality.

"Why are we here though?" said Davy " I mean it's been interesting hearing what happened to us all but, you know, are we doing some ghost laying ?"

"Oh Davy" said Sarah, " Yes, I think that's it. After Gideon's funeral, well I looked through lots of stuff and I have brought a few bits with me from those days, mainly photographs"

"Yes, me too" said Jane

"I found a box a few months ago, among the stuff I had brought here from my mothers and never got round to dealing with" said Leon

"It said 1968 on the lid and it was full of all sorts of papers mainly, fliers and pamphlets and old newspapers, letters a few photos. God knows why I'd kept it. That's really why I came to the funeral, a week after I'd found it and put it to one side to look through I got Claire's email about Gideon's death"

"How odd," said Sarah. "Will you show us?"

"Yes, tomorrow maybe, I don't think I'm up to it now" replied Leon. They started to talk about the next day, time of breakfast, what they might do. The weather was set fair, June had been marvellous so far. Leon spoke of Saxon churches, of open gardens, of Aldeburgh nearby, Davy sipped his whisky and thought how he really had drunk too much. Jane thought how nice Leon had made his house and worried about the obvious newness of the sheets on their bed. Sarah thought about the contents of the box that Leon had found . Leon thought with weariness how different it was having a full house instead of just him and his ginger cat.

Finally, just before midnight they all made their way to bed.

. Chapter 15: Suffolk Day 2

Jane was no longer used to sharing a bed with Howard and his hot and bulky form beside her had caused her a night of fitful sleep. When Tommy, their eldest, left university a few years before and got his own flat in Hackney she had started sleeping in his bedroom, to Howard´s remonstrance she had sited night sweats, broken sleep, wanting to read in the middle of the night. After a while it became routine rather than occasional and the year before she had finally decorated the room, made new curtains, bought herself a new single bed.

 When she finally awoke fully it was from a dream of Gideon, he had been coming towards her, waving and smiling, she was running to him and then realised he was looking past her, she turned and there was Marina, Marina in an enormous black hat which hid her face. As Marina got closer Jane saw under the brim of the hat was a grinning skull. That was when she woke, heart thudding, tears choking her throat. She lay breathing deeply to calm herself, looking at her watch she saw it was 5a.m. She had not dreamt of Gideon for years, it must be being here, with the others, the funeral and everything she told herself.

Finally, at 6a.m, when it was light and she could hear the distant sound of cockerels she decided to get up and make a cup of tea. Putting a cardigan over her nightdress she went quietly downstairs.

Opening the door into the kitchen she was surprised to see Leon already there, he appeared to be kneading dough. Farming Today was playing quietly on the radio in the background

"o, sorry" she said:

 "Is it alright if I make a cup of tea?'

"Yes, of course," said Leon. They did not speak, Jane made a pot, poured a mug for herself and another for Leon and made to go.

"Is Howard still asleep?" asked Leon.

: YES' said Jane.

"Well, have your tea here, I don't mind, I'll just get on"

"Thanks" Jane sat, sipping her tea, it was calming to watch Leon buttering the loaf tins, kneading the dough into shape and then covering the tins with clean tea towels.

After a while she said

"I dreamt about Gideon and Marina, a disturbing dream, it woke me"

"Well, they were a disturbing pair," said Leon.

"I was so young and stupid back then," said Jane. "I sometimes think what happened shaped my whole life".

Leon looked directly at her, taking in her still dark hair, only slightly streaked with silver, tousled by sleep, the fine lines around her eyes and mouth, the still dream haunted look in her dark eyes.

 "Well, yes" he said after a short silence "I think it changed us all, certainly it affected me, Paul was such a sweet man, I think that was why I went off travelling, could not make sense of it, why him, you know"

"Hmm, I loved him "said Jane, tears filling her eyes for her long ago self and her cherished comforter.

"He was so kind to me when I was in such a mess over Gideon. I was so stupid, so naïve'

"Jane" said Leon gently, noticing her fists clenched in her lap "You were young. We were young, we knew nothing and thought we knew everything. It's the past, you have a life, a family, a solid marriage, more than a lot of people"

Jane thought about Howard, no doubt snoring upstairs, thought of her desire for babies, surely a desire to make up for the abortion, for the need for a safe haven after the pain and turbulence. A solid comforting presence, one who barely knew what she had been through, he took her back to the Jane she had been before Gideon. When he asked her to marry him it seemed inevitable, her family, who had been so worried about her that last summer were delighted and the babies followed thick and fast. Those busy years, and her part time teaching job gave her little time for introspection but now they had all flown the nest and it was just Howard and her. She sometimes wondered what her life might have been, who else she might have become.

Thinking of Howard, she got up and sighing said

 "Oh well, of course you are right, that was the past, this is the present, being here in your lovely house with all the others, time to get on. I'll take Howard up a cup of tea and get dressed."

Sarah was the next down, dressed in jeans and a floral shirt, ready for the day. Warm smells of baking bread greeted her, she saw the back door was open, no one about, so she took her tea outside to drink it and the huge soft blue Suffolk sky with equal appreciation.

After a while Leon appeared from the bottom of the garden with more raspberries and a clutch of carrots.
"It's so nice here Leon" said Sarah."'Thanks again for inviting us all"
 "Well, actually I don't know what came over me" said Leon.
"I lead a pretty solitary life here. You are my first guests."
He had bought the house on a whim 10 years before, was in England for debriefings from his last posting in Novi Sad, had gone to Aldeburgh for the Festival and idly looking in estate agent's windows had seen the house, neglected with a large garden at an affordable price. With vague thoughts of retirement, a place for the future he had bought it. Over the intervening years when on leave in England he had altered it, extended and repaired, begun to lay out a garden. Now the garden had become a surprising and absorbing passion and the house was comfortable and suited him perfectly.
Jane and Howard were down next, a breakfast of new bread, fruit and yoghurt and muesli was placed on the table. Howard, who liked a fry up at weekends, looked askance at the spread but cheered up when Leon said he thought a pub lunch and a look about Aldeburgh was a possible plan for the day. Jane and Howard had never been there and Sarah only once for a concert at Snape Maltings, part of an unsatisfactory weekend with an unsatisfactory lover twenty years before so they all readily agreed. Half way through breakfast a rumpled Davy appeared and he too liked the plan.

So, they set off in two cars, Jane and Howard in their car with Sarah and Leon and Davy in Leon's Citroen.

Aldeburgh exerted its charm on them all, a visit to the Maltings was included and a potter around the charming very high-end tourist shops After a busy morning it was with happy relief that they all settled around a round table in the garden of a big pub with a sea view.

Over lunch Sarah said

"By the way Leon, I noticed two charming little water colours on the landing, I thought they might be India? One I think was of you?"

"Yes" said Davy, 'you were there for a few years after Brighton, weren't you?

"oh, I must look" said Jane

"So what's the story Leon?" asked Sarah.

Leon hesitated,

"Actually Marina painted them"

"What!" spluttered Davy, spilling wine down his front.

"Marina?" Said Jane and Sarah together.

"Not Marina the white witch," laughed Howard.

"How come? "said Davy

Leon told them briefly of the three days he and Marina had spent together in Varanasi in 1972 and the pictures she had left behind.

"I was going back to England after two years away, I was spending my last few weeks in Varanasi and a couple of days before I left I met her, she literally stumbled upon me sitting by the Ghats"

The rest of the lunch was, inevitably, spent talking about Marina. Davy, who had always stayed in contact with Gideon, they were, after all boyhood friends, reminded them that at the end of the third year Gideon had gone to California to join Marina for the summer of love

. "Oh dear" said Sarah, "of course, she always wanted to be at the centre of things and didn't her mother live in California?'

"Yes, and the film Gideon made there was his entrée into the BBC training scheme, that and his film about Les Eventements in Paris, May 68."

Both Sarah and Leon cast quick glances at Jane, that was the month of horrors for her, for them all except Gideon and Marina, blithely skimming the excitement wherever it was.

"I think she came to India after that, you know, she never talked about herself but she was damaged when we hooked up"

"I wonder what happened to her?" mused Jane "I was so scared of her back then"

Howard looked at her with surprise, there was a tremor in her voice, she was inadvertently shredding her paper napkin.

"Well changing the subject "he said, "that was a great lunch but I could do with a nap now" he had eaten and drunk more than the rest of them, ordering a second bottle of wine, most of which he drank. Sarah wanted to see the Maggie Hambling sculpture on the shore, Davy wanted to browse a couple of book shops so it was agreed Sarah would borrow the Citroen and Leon would go back with Jane and Howard. Leon wanted to get on with some gardening and Jane thought she would like some quiet time in Leon's garden, she felt a bit unsettled and a bit anxious. They settled the bill with some wrangling but in the end Davy and Howard split it and they parted, each to their afternoons.

When Howard, Jane and Leon got back to Leon's house Howard and Jane went up to their room. Leon said he was going to put in a bit of time in the garden. Howard collapsed on the bed, having first taken off his shoes and was soon asleep. Jane quietly pottered around their room, she retrieved a folder, neatly marked Brighton Days, from her case, collected her book, an Elizabeth Strout, and set off downstairs. She paused on the landing, remembering the pictures Sarah had mentioned in the pub. There they were, two watercolours, one of a young man, sitting cross legged in a landscape of curious tombs, , the other a bare room with the outline of a figure in the narrow bed, covered by a cotton spread, all you could see was a tangle of red hair on a flat pillow. Jane breathed sharply, yes of course, that was her, was Marina ,though barely sketched.

She went down into the garden, first putting her folder on the table in the sitting room. She noticed that Leon had tidied up from the previous night, glasses and bottles gone. She recalled how fastidious he had been at St Agnes Avenue, exasperated with the mess Davy left when he cooked. There was a laptop on the table and beside it a box labelled 1968/9. Resisting the urge to look inside she went out into the garden.

No sign of Leon so she took one of the garden chairs to under a spreading lilac tree and settled down to read.

Quite soon her thoughts wandered, had it been worth coming here? Would ghosts be laid as Davy had laughingly said at Gideon's funeral? It was fun seeing Davy and Sarah was part of her life , always a good friend. Leon was the surprise, the ascetic loner settled in this lovely house, still reserved but she felt connected to him ,his presence was peaceful but alert.

Just then he appeared,"Always weeding to do " he said, dragging over a chair to beside her.

"Tell me about it" she laughed

She looked at her watch,

"Maybe time for tea?" They spoke over each other

"How about tea?" said Leon. Laughing Jane got up,

"I´ll make it you go and wash"

So they reprised their early morning cup of tea, though now a day had passed, in mainly inconsequential chatter but an intimacy had tentatively been established.

"I looked at Marina's pictures' said Jane, "they are very good"

"Yes" said Leon. "She was in a very disturbed place when we met. India and goodness knows what else had got to her, she was on edge, angry, but then she was always angry"

"oh, " said Jane," did you think so? I always thought of her as superior, above all emotion somehow, so careless of people"

"I think all that, the way she was, was what she presented to the world to hide her misery and insecurity When we talked in India she said how she hated us all, that we were all so superior"

"Us? Me? Sarah??? ' said Jane in disbelief.

"One thing I have learnt, Jane, is that we are many people in our lives, when we are young we are trying selves on , if we have felt unloved, unwanted, we try harder maybe to force people to love us and if we do not know how to do that to fear us or even dislike us but a reaction, a connection is what we need"

Jane was silent, considering what he had said.

There was the sound of a car, then doors slammed and Sarah and Davy came around the back of the house.

"Here you are," said Sarah. " We've had a great time, we made a detour to Southwold, I'd read about the crazy pier there, such fun, "

"Yeh, it was great, really clever and witty automata," said Davy, plonking himself down.

"Any chance of tea?"

Chattering about what they had seen, about Maggie Hambling's magnificent shell on the beach, they went into the kitchen followed by Leon and Jane. Leon made fresh tea and Jane took a cup up to Howard.

"Supper at 8 "said Leon, "oh and I've put some things in the sitting room"

" So have I" added Jane. "Stuff from the past, we can have a look after supper"

"Oh, good, I found a few pictures and fliers" said Sarah , 'I will bring them down'.

"Afraid I travel light, too many wives and moves' laughed Davy "but the last time I saw Gideon he gave me a folder of photographs of the band, I brought them with me."

"Great" said Sarah. She had enjoyed her day, Davy had always made her laugh and her sprits were high

" I'm just in the mood for looking back" she turned to Jane, "You'll see it will be fun"

She knew her friend, knew she must have reservations but also knew that Jane had worked through those troubling days.

Chapter 16: The evening

Leon had bought a large salmon quiche and various cold meats from Waitrose in Aldeburgh, had dug up new potatoes from the garden . He, Jane and Sarah assembled a huge bowl of salad, mixed leaves, tiny tomatoes, olives, rocket, radishes, cucumber, all home grown , decorated with nasturtium flowers. He took some roasted peppers out of the oven and said

"Well, we can help ourselves I think"

"Wow" ' said Davy, getting out his mobile phone "Must send a picture of this spread to Janine, she likes to use flowers in food, she'll be impressed my English chums do too."

"How different it is than from when we were young" mused Sarah

"If we had only had mobile phones so many cockups and dramas would not have happened"

"Yes" said Davy "So much time wasted looking for people trying to arrange things"

"Hmm" Leon finished putting plates on the table,

"But a much better pace of life, surely? Many of the places I have worked had very poor signals, and communication networks generally so we had to rely on meeting up, being where we said we would be, allowing time for delays"

Howard lumbered in, catching the end of the conversation, he had been on his laptop in the sitting room, catching up on emails and deals:

"Not my world mate" he said, "finance only works because of global instant communication."

He looked at the table

"Oh good" he said " I'm ready for some rabbit food"

"Ignore him" said Jane, "It all looks lovely"

Davy produced a bottle of champagne,

" Got this in Southwold, thought we could have a toast, seeing as how we've all made it this far"

There were general noises of assent and pleasure and

"Lovely" said Sarah "To us, to the present and to our shared past"

They clinked glasses, drank deep and helped themselves to food. By common consent they wandered into the sitting room with their plates. The windows were open on to the garden, there was a gentle breeze, the heat of the day was passing. Spread out on a big round table in the corner were several folders, a box, an untidy pile of photographs.

Leon said "I thought we could all have a rifle through maybe, after we've eaten."

They all settled down, enjoying the fresh food. Davy opened his lap top and said 'Let's have some memory music"
and next thing Bob Dylan's croaky inimitable voice was singing, the backdrop of so many nights at St Agnes Avenue.
Gradually, as they finished eating they drifted over to the table....Sarah was first and called Jane over, she had opened Leon's box marked `Brighton´
"O my god! Look at us!" first out was a photograph of the three of them, Jane, Sarah and Marina in incredibly short black dresses, off the shoulder, fishnet tights, knee high black boots, long hair tumbling, black, blond and red ,
" It's the Ranters!"   Davy came to look.
" Wow, god yes, you girls were really hot stuff back then !"
Sarah gave him a sharp nudge
 'Well yes, different days Davy"
Howard said " Lets see" reaching out a hand from the armchair he was wedged in. Davy passed it over
" Bloody hell Jane" he said, " I'd forgotten that side of you"
Jane blushed, that cursed blush, glanced over at Leon who was sitting by the window
"Oh dear, "she laughed, embarrassed, "What would the children say?"
"God yes, Mary would die laughing" said Sarah ruefully.
 "Yes," said Leon "The young never believe the old were young once" he pushed aside the other stuff on the table and lifted out the

contents of the box

" I'd left this at my mother's when I left England, had quite forgotten about it and when she died I brought it here with some of her furniture, haven't really looked at it."

Spread over the table were yellowing copies of International Times with lurid psychedelic covers, Friends magazine, Oz, Rolling Stone, Red Mole, piles of inky leaflets for demos, pamphlets, manifestos , some Ranters posters, posters for gigs, Jimi Hendrix, Pink Floyd, Cream, one for Mick Jagger's free concert in Hyde Park in 1969.

" God Leon, a treasure trove for a 60's researcher" laughed Davy. He collected a pile of papers, topped up his wine glass and settled down to read. Sarah did likewise. Howard continued to slumber and Jane sat on the chair beside him half reading a pamphlet on the Cultural Revolution . There was quite a bit of Maoist stuff in the box and anti war in Vietnam leaflets, newspaper reports about the storming of the American embassy in Grosvenor Square. She picked up this and nudged Howard, a bit embarrassed at how disengaged he was ,

" Howard, wake up. Do you remember this" she showed him the picture in the news report from Peace News,

"Ohuh, my finest hour, hey Davy look at this.."

Davy came over and looked at the cutting, then Howard googled Grosvenor Square demo March 1968 and up came a pile of entries and some YouTube videos. He clicked on one and they all came over to look, the police, the crowds, the anger, the shock, all caught and preserved .

They talked over each other, Davy reminiscing about his night in the police cells, "Gave me cred with my students' ' he said, Sarah still bemoaning the Biba jacket the police tore off her as Howard dragged her to safety from the horse's hooves. Jane, still horrified at the poor horses ,whacked by demonstrators and police alike, and her first realisation of the power of the state.

Leon fetched a 3rd bottle of wine from the kitchen. Jane got up and neatly stacking the papers from Leon's box, unearthed a battered pale green folder. Davy had brought this, given him by Gideon not long before he died. It said The Ranters in faded ink on the front. "Do you remember" he said,

"Marina and Gideon took lots of photos, especially Marina, she talked of an art project, or blowing them up for posters, she and Gideon used to argue over the camera, it was a good one she borrowed from the art school, or possibly stole, who knows, she seemed to have it most gigs" said Davy.

Whilst he was talking Sarah had joined Jane at the table, was looking through them, stopped for a minute over one then pushed it under the others. Howard, who had joined them said

"What's that?",and extracted the picture.

"Ha, soft porn eh?"

It was a picture of a naked Marina, in profile, in all her extraordinary beauty, gazing out of the window in the big front bedroom at ST Agnes avenue, one hand was lifting her heavy red hair off the back of her neck, her breasts were raised, her pose balletic and totally self absorbed. The image was both tender and oddly unsettling.

"O god" said Davy, " she was lovely. You know she would turn up like that in my room sometimes." He paused ,lost in reminiscence and Sarah said

"You bugger! I always thought there was something between you"

"Not really" said Davy, shaking his head in remembered bewilderment,

" She never said much, just ,you know, got into bed"

Jane was listening to this exchange with bemusement, Marina and Davy? Marina creeping up to the attic when Gideon was asleep? Why?

" OH I never understood her ,she seemed to operate according to a totally different set of rules from everyone else" she said .

Leon had been listening ,

'It doesn´t really surprise me" he said " Her sexuality gave her power, and maybe she felt powerless, her fucked up childhood and everything"

Sarah nodded her head thoughtfully

" It's true, back then many young women only had sex as currency, before sisterhood, feminism, gay rights"

Meanwhile Howard had been studying the picture, he nudged Davy "Lucky sod, nice surprise when it happened eh?"

"Give it to me, Howard "said Jane quietly. Quickly glancing at it she put it back in the folder and Leon, to cover the sudden tension said

" What are the rest?" They pored over the photos, there were lots of them all playing, several of Gideon alone, a great one of Leon and Davy playing their guitars, close together and smiling, a picture of the three girls in skin tight red mini dresses, high boots again, Jane looked thinner, somehow much wilder and then, a picture, a beautiful close up of Paul, blond hair flopping across his face at his drums, sticks raised and with a huge ecstatic smile.

Jane reached blindly for Sarah "O Sarah, that's the last gig, I remember those ridiculous dresses, it's the night Paul died." And she shuddered, sank onto the sofa and put her head in her hands. Nobody spoke, in the background Procul Harem were playing A whiter Shade of Pale, Jane was transported back to that awful day when she found Paul's body. After a silence, Leon spoke

" I have always felt guilty about his death" said Leon ," I could see he was on a road to self destruction , but I did nothing"

"O mate" said Davy gruffly,

" It was me that kept him supplied with pills, I didn't realise how much he was drinking, I have carried that too"

" But me , if only I had checked in on him earlier, I bear most of the blame," said Jane in a choked voice. She was just keeping herself together, Howard patted her arm but she pushed him away

" I really loved him" she said " he was so sweet to me, understood how I felt about Gideon , comforted me night after night after the abortion" the words gushed out of her.

" What ? What abortion? What are you talking about?" said Howard, suddenly alert.

" Leave it Howard" said Sarah

"No, I won't, what else haven't you told me about ? What abortion? Was it that bastard Gideon's ?" demanded Howard.

Leon said "Howard, this is all 40 odd years ago, no point in being upset now."

The tensions and undercurrents of the last 36 hours ,the large amount he had drunk, his unarticulated feeling of being excluded, so well remembered from the Ranters days ,flooded over Howard.

"Well you can fuck off, I'm talking to my wife, what Janey?"

Jane looked up at his red sweating face, insensitive, boorish Howard, the father of her children, her big mistake, her safe haven after Gideon but also her prison.

" I don't want to talk about it, Howard. Why don't you just go to bed and leave me alone?" Jane spoke forcefully for her and Howard glowered,

" Oh yes, you and your Brighton lot, only time you were alive eh? Always second best, I know, I know and I'm sick of it. All of you, always looked down on me..just good old Howard ,man with a van" he spluttered, looked around " Yes I will go to bed…you wankers, you all thought you were so fucking cool" he spat out the last word and stumbled from the room leaving an appalled silence behind him.

Jane, ever good mannered ,said " oh I am so sorry, he's been under strain at work lately, we haven't been close for a long while , he resents it I know, thinks I'm cold, gets fed up" she trailed to a stop, looked instinctively for Sarah who came and put her arms around her.

After an uneasy silence where all that was heard was soft music,

Dylan again, Davy said

" Well I suppose it was true what he said . we all totally took him for granted"

Ever practical Sarah said dismissively

" Too much to drink. Anyone for a cup of tea?"

Leon got to his feet, started tidying up,

" Whisky for me, a nightcap in bed " said Davy and then

' God Janine would kill me if she knew how much I've been drinking. She only allows me two glasses of wine a day "

Sarah went into the kitchen, Jane pulled herself together and started to collect the plates from their supper. Leon said

" Leave that'

" No I want to, I'm ok, honestly".

Carrying the dirty plates they went into the kitchen. Sarah said to Jane

"You ok love? We can talk tomorrow, I think I'll take my tea up"

Sarah left and Leon and Jane were alone in the kitchen.

Jane went outside with her tea, looking up at the night sky, breathing deeply to calm herself , becoming aware of the night scents of the garden. She could hear Leon pottering about in the kitchen. With a mixture of fear and elation she suddenly realised clearly that she should leave Howard. It was almost five years since Gareth, their youngest child, had finally left home, and slowly and imperceptibly she and Howard had ceased to have any real connection. He worked long hours, had his clubs that he went to 'to meet some chaps" she gardened, worked, wrote poetry These days mostly elegiac, regretful

, yearning for something unknown. She filled her days with busyness and grandchildren but felt an emptiness at the centre of herself. She sighed deeply, and just then Leon came outside.

"Are you alright Jane?" he asked

She smiled ruefully

"Well yes and no" she said

" Do you want to talk?" Asked Leon, surprising himself, usually he was wary of emotions, kept his distance but Jane had always touched him somewhere deep inside, her mixture of modesty and compassion. He had always known she was the cleverest of all of them but the one who least advertised the fact. The First she got was no surprise when he heard nor her modest success with her poetry but she was self deprecating, was quiet about anything she had published.

He waited and after a minute she said

" Since Gideon's funeral I have been thinking about the time we all lived together, inevitable ,but tonight, when I saw that picture of Paul….." she paused, " well it seemed like yesterday, and for a minute I felt the guilt and shame all over again. It was all mixed up in my mind with Gideon,the band, my abortion ,'

"Shame?" asked Leon quietly.

" Yes ,because that Jane back then wasn't me. Ever since I first saw Gideon I wanted to be what he wanted, I did things, behaved in ways, accepted things, just to keep him, and the irony was it was all pointless because he was Marina's"

Leon was quiet for a few moments

" I don't know " he said eventually " I don't think anybody held Gideon. He used Marina, for her contacts, for her beauty, I don't think he cared about her really. Gideon only cared about himself, his ambition to be famous, whatever it took"

'Hmm, perhaps you're right. I don't know but what I have been slowly realising is I married Howard and had the babies as a direct consequence of all that happened. I mourned my lost baby, flushed down the toilet at St Agnes avenue, I was frightened as to where emotion and passion had led me, Howard was familiar, safe, kind, I just retreated from the world and now, at last I am waking up. I want something more, I look at Sarah's life, she is so secure, so happy now and independent, I want that for myself."

After a silence Leon said

" Funerals, always ,at our age, cause us to take stock, think about what we have achieved, wonder how long we have got left. I guess we ask ourselves do we want to end our days full of what might have beens, or use the time we have left to the fullest?"

Jane stood up, walked to stand under the lilac and inhale its blossom then she turned and said

""'Thank you Leon. Thank you for being you, listening and thank you for how kind you were in the days after Paul's death before I finally retreated home. I have not forgotten, how could I, that it was you who brought me round when I tried" she could not say it but continued" "when I was so stupid, you saved my life'

"Well maybe, " said Leon " bad times"

The pair of them sat for a while in silence, each wrapped in their own thoughts. Eventually Jane got up

" I think I will suggest to Howard he drives home in the morning and I will go back to London on the train with Davy and Sarah, maybe go back to Bristol with Sarah. I need some time alone I think"

" Whatever you think best , said Leon neutrally ."Good night then, sleep well

Jane and Howard came down to the kitchen early, whatever had passed between them had left Howard subdued and gruffly apologetic

' Sorry about last night old man," he said to Leon "Too much to drink, no excuse but think might as well get off, leave you four to yourselves"

Jane looked at him, was that a slight dig she wondered. He quickly swallowed a cup of tea from the pot on the table and said he would pick up breakfast on the way. He went out into the hall and picked up his case,

" Say goodbye to Sarah and Davy" he said and with an automatic peck on Jane's cheek was off.

Jane went back into the kitchen and poured herself a cup of tea, Leon was busy getting out breakfast things

"Everything alright?" he asked.

"Yes" said Jane quietly, "I suppose so, poor Howard"

Leon said nothing and then began to talk about what they might do this sunny Sunday. Davy and Sarah were catching the 4 o'clock train, Jane too now.

"I think I would like a walk" she said, so Leon went and collected the OS map of the area and Jane spread it on the table.

Sarah came down, was told Howard had gone. She helped herself to some muesli, fruit and yoghurt and discussed a walk with Jane "That would be so nice" she said "and we can have a proper talk" By the time Davy appeared Jane and Sarah were putting on their walking boots, Davy said "Oh I'm quite happy to stay here, perhaps we could pick up the Sunday papers Leon and I will sit in the garden."

"No problem "said Leon "and I think I will get on with some gardening then. You two will be ok?'

"Of course" laughed Sarah, "we are both competent map readers. We'll see you in a couple of hours."

Sarah and Jane did not talk at all at first, they were used to each other's company, were at ease with being silent together. Sarah guessed that Jane had a lot to process and waited for her to begin, enjoying the sounds and smells of the Suffolk countryside. Eventually Jane said

"I think I am ready to grow up, I have more or less decided to leave Howard"

"O Jane, that is major" said Sarah " I know you lead pretty separate lives but what about security, future old age,Are you sure?, "

Jane stopped in her tracks and looked at her friend

"Do you think about those things?"

Sarah hesitated "No not really, I live as much as I can in the present"

"Well then. I have realised that all my choices since ST Agnes Avenue have been about security and safety and now I find myself at this great age in a companionate marriage where we have nothing in common except three children. I feel stifled, I feel as if there is nothing much ahead except more of the same and that's
not what I want"

Sarah made a noise of agreement

"I see, so what brought this on? Last night's outburst? The photos?"

"I suppose so, that girl I was in the band, she is in me somewhere. I do not mean the pathetic lovelorn girl but the one who took risks, joined a band, went on demos, made friends with a wild girl from Bristol" she stopped and gave Sarah a hug.

" You have always been an inspiration to me Sarah, and I see how happy you are now with your move to Bristol, you've always lead an independent life. I have always been dependent on Howard. I know I am much cleverer than him" she shot a glance at Sarah, " I know this sounds vain but I got used to deferring to him, allowing him to take charge. When he took charge of everything, after Paul's death, I was so grateful to him. He was so calm and competent ,he really was a shelter in the storm" she laughed ruefully " and he was good with the children, a good father it's just now I want another life"

Everything Jane said, Sarah had thought privately over the years. Sometimes she had been exasperated with what she saw as Jane's passivity, wondered if she would ever assert herself. After a bit she said

"Jane, my dear dear friend, whatever you do I will support you and I want you to know I think you are absolutely right"

Jane burst into tears, the two of them stopped dead in the middle of the lane, one laughing and the other crying.

Jane said "Oh I feel as if a great suffocating blanket has lifted off me"

The rest of their walk was discussions around how to handle Howard, what the house in Muswell Hill was worth, how the children would react. By the time they got back to Leon's they were both giddy with plans and possibilities.

Sarah threw herself into one of the garden chairs beside Davy and eased off her boots. Jane went upstairs to wash her face and take a few minutes. Sarah, as always, had been supportive but her total embrace of Jane's tentative plans had been a bit overwhelming. Davy and Sarah had been joined by Leon and the three of them were sipping cold beers. She got herself a glass of water and joined them,

"We were just discussing what we should do for lunch" said Leon" There is a nice pub in the village or we could drive to Dunwich and have fish and chips from the beach cafe"

"Oh yes, said Jane " if we are near the sea we should have fish and chips."

They started to reminisce about the Trip Out Cafe, which had done brilliant fish and chips. Sarah, Jane and Davy had spent a lot of time there in their last year at Brighton.

They all managed to fit into Leon's Citroen Diane and had a pleasant time, exploring the drowned village and relishing the delicious fish and chips. As three o'clock approached they headed back to Leon's to collect their luggage and get to the station, Jane needed to buy a ticket so they had to get there a bit early. Leon drove them all and they had time to stand around making their good byes .

"Well" said Davy "It's been really good catching up, you have a lovely place and great to see you again after all these years Leon"

"Keep in touch Jane" Leon said quietly "let me know how things go" He kissed the two women and shook Davy's hand and they climbed on the half empty train.

The train pulled out, Leon watched until it disappeared and then walked back to his car. He felt drained, partly from the tensions of Saturday night, partly from being with other people when used to being on his own and finally, he realised, with the feelings that had resurfaced from so long ago which he had always held for Jane.

Chapter 17: 3years later

It was early spring and Jane had spent the afternoon planting primulas and violas under the big old lime tree in the corner of her garden. As so often when she was gardening Jane's thoughts roamed over the last few years of momentous change.

She had moved into her three-bedroom cottage at Blagden Lake, a convenient half an hour from Bristol and Sarah, two years before. She was finally beginning to feel pleased with the garden, a good size and south facing.

The divorce from Howard had been remarkably easy, after a few months of hurt and bluster it emerged that he, ever conventional, had been having an affair with his secretary, Helen, for the last five years. Jane liked her, she had worked for Howard for fifteen years and, now, approaching late middle age herself, was more than willing to swap the role of mistress for wife. Selling up the big family house in Muswell Hill had netted a tidy sum, enough for Jane to buy her cottage, for Howard and Helen to buy an apartment in Maida Vale and for each of the three children to be given 20 thousand. This had gone a long way to help reconcile them to the surprising turn of events, the sudden resolve and actions of their mother.

Molly, their daughter, who loved and admired Sarah went down to Bristol for the day, leaving her children with Jane, to talk it over and see if Sarah thought her mother really wanted this. After that visit she became totally supportive of her mother, realising it was high time that she lived her own life. Tommy, the eldest, once he had clarified that his mother would still be available for help with childcare, would come up and stay if needed, even if she did move out of London, also eventually accepted the news. Gareth, the youngest, was the most bewildered but Molly and Tommy gave him a good talking to and, since he was passionate about fishing and realised that his mother was moving to a village near the famous Blagdon fishing Lake he had soon become a regular visitor, leaving his rods at his mother's.

Jane saw Sarah regularly, had, at her instigation, started to work one day a week at the Refugee Crisis Centre in Bristol where Sarah gave legal advice. She acted as a befriender and taught English language classes. Her skill, sympathy and gentleness made her popular and she got immense satisfaction from the work. She was also writing a lot and, as so many times in the long ago past, she sent the poems she was working on to Leon.

Picking up her trowel and gardening gloves she walked towards the house. Time for a cup of tea, she thought. She was so glad to have this new life, a new life at 70. Her own life to live just as she wanted. In the last three years she had become a regular visitor to Suffolk, a couple of times with Sarah, once with Davy and Janine but usually on her own. Leon came to stay with her too and their friendship was deepening in a way warming and interesting to them both. The three of them, Sarah, Jane and Leon, were planning a trip to France to stay with Davy and Janine for Easter. Davy had had a minor heart attack two years before and Janine had firmly curtailed his trips to London, he now came over much less frequently but when he did Sarah would go up to meet him. She would come back from these outings full of more than usual joie de vivre, "Davy is such good company" she would say as she regaled Jane with his latest exploits.

   As she went down the side path to the back door she heard the phone ringing. Hurrying in she picked up the phone.
" Jane, it's me Sarah ,have you checked your emails lately?"
"No I've been gardening"
 "Quick look now at the one from Davy, then phone me ok?"
"yes ok" laughed Jane.
She stopped to make herself a cup of tea then went into the sitting room and opened her laptop;

To Jane/Sarah/Leon date April 3rd
Subject: MARINA

Hi guys,
Blast from the past!Janine has just come back from an exhibition in Paris, talk of the town. An artist called Mariana Neuf who was formerly ……MARINA LASCELLES..our Marina!. She has also written a book `From Chaos to Calm, My Journey` which Janine bought. I'll get her to translate and send some bits before you all come. How about that then. ? Marina resurfaces, remade!!!"
Love Davy

Jane rang Sarah and they agreed to try googling her and to wait for Davy's next email. Then Jane rang Leon to mull it over with him. .

To Jane/Sarah/Leon   Date April 6th

Subject Marina/Mariana

Mariana Neuf formerly Marina Lascelles b 1947

Mother: The Hon Henrietta Lascelles……..!!!

Father :Vicomte Charles du Fournay …….!!

Parents married 1945 divorced 1950

Education :   1953-1965 Various english progressive boarding schools, brief period in a convent School. Expelled 5 times

      1966-1968   Brighton art School

      1972-1974   Ecole de arte superior Paris

      1968-1971   California……………summer of love and all that LSD etc

      1970-1972 India ……………..that's when you met her Leon

      1974-1985   Worked for and with Andy Warhol, part of his entourage!!!!!

And then 1985..epiphany. Janine hasn't got to that part yet but here's a couple of good quotes

"I spent 30 years losing myself,10 years finding myself and the last 10 years helping others find themselves" [oh yeh?]

And

"I was a total bitch, I hated everyone and myself most of all. I despised women, I manipulated and despised men because they were so easy to manipulate,I was promiscuous, lied, stole, cheated. took excessive amounts of drugs, had 2 spells in rehab

And then in 1985 I met a woman who set me on a new path which I have followed ever since. I am a Lesbian, a teetotaller ,a vegan and I practise yoga and Tai chi. I have reached a calm and safe shore at last."

Well!!! What can I say? She certainly kept her posh background quiet tho does not surprise me. Anyway, LOTS to discuss. See you all next week, a bientot, love Davy

Sarah on the phone to Jane
" An Hon!!! A vicomte!"

Jane : Andy Warhol!"

Sarah: "rehab!"

Jane :"a lesbian"

Sarah :"despised women..stole

Jane " yes, your red skirt!"

Sarah " Fancy you remember that"

They carried on talking for some time, trying to match these snippets with the Marina they had known. And then Jane rang Leon to talk it over some more. Leon, on one of their weekends, had told Jane more about the three days he had spent with a distraught and disturbed Marina in Varanassi in 1972. He said that he was not surprised at her story.

" Marina always wanted to be at the heart of the action,Paris 68, California,hippy trail, Warhol seemed a natural progression. And no wonder she hated everyone, she had been rejected over and over, all those boarding schools, from aged six ,imagine Jane?

"From six? " said Jane.

"Yes ,it said from 1953," said Leon.

Jane thought of her own children at six , so little, so tender and vulnerable, sending them off, then spending the holidays in 2 different countries, being rejected by five schools, even progressive ones.

"I guess her expulsions was her acting out,needing love and not finding it " she said .

"I'm glad she's found peace at last"

Chapter 18: France, Easter

The three friends traveled together on the ferry to Roscoff. Davy was at the port to meet them and they took a leisurely drive back through the green Breton countryside.

"Oh Davy, it's so nice to be on holiday" said Sarah and the others happily agreed. Primulas were flowering in the hedgerows and chestnut and larch trees hung over the road sides Eventually they arrived in Poulenoc where Janine was waiting in the porch of a granite-built cottage, typical of the region. What was different was a large glass walled studio built on the side and behind it what appeared to be an annexe to the main house. Janine was plump, had thick blond grey hair pinned up with shell combs and was wearing a loose pink smock, heavy wooden beads and Capri trousers in a vivid green.

"Well" she said, smiling broadly,

" So happy you are all here, at last you come to our house. Welcome ,I will tell you first your rooms."

"You will be here Leon" indicating the studio,

"And Sarah and Jane, I hope it is ok to share? It is a big room, upstairs with a bathroom"

"Oh it's all lovely" said Jane, taking in the pictures on the walls on the way upstairs, watercolours, pastels, paintings all hung higgeldy piggeldy some landscapes, some portraits, a glorious wall.

The bedroom she and Sarah were to share was the width of the upstairs, a door on one wall led into the bathroom, a large window looked out onto fields, lots more paintings hung on the walls and beautiful textiles were thrown over the bed and the generous sofa under the window. There was a vase of daffodils on the old chest of drawers and a large dark wooden armoire on another wall. A small shelf held a collection of oddly shaped stones.

"Oh, it's perfect " said Jane

"Thank you so much, merci beaucoup, for having us all" said Sarah

"Well, if I will not let my wicked Davy go to London so much I must allow him have his friends here"

Davy had followed them up the stairs and hearing Janine's last remark he gave her a slap on her spreading bottom and blowing her a kiss said

"Oh ho, you can see she is the boss, ok. So how about you sort yourselves out and then I think it is warm enough to sit outside"

Janine smiled at him affectionately,

"Yes and soon I must get on with the dinner, so we leave you"

"Oh, she's so lovely " said Jane when they had gone.

She and Sarah had speculated about what sort of woman would have managed to tame Davy, Janine was plump and maternal with a warm sexuality and a direct gaze which was very attractive. She also was clearly committed to her work just as Davy was.

They talked for a bit longer, unpacked, chose who had which bed and then went downstairs to the kitchen. It was a big untidy room, more pictures on the walls, a big noticeboard with torn out newspaper articles, tickets, postcards, invitations to gallery openings. The whole of one side was an oven and there were racks of pans, shelves of bowls and china and kitchen equipment. Davy had said Janine was a keen cook and her kitchen was clear evidence.

"Welcome to my laboratory' said Janine as they came in

" As you see, I love to cook and to experiment. Leon is outside with Davy. What would you like now? An aperitif? Tea, perhaps? I know you English like a nice cup of tea "

"Oh, tea for me please" said Jane laughing and Sarah chose an aperitif.

" After all" she said " it's 5 o'clock" Janine looked a bit baffled at this

"Is there a right time?'

Sarah laughed "No I guess not for some!"

"So, I will bring it, you go and find them'

The two of them went out into the garden, a path led to a small orchard where they could see the men sitting at a table.

"Hi, everything ok?" asked Davy, watching them approach .

"It's perfect, what a nice place you have here" said Sarah

"Yes well, its Janine's old family home, belonged to her grandmother" said Davy

"Just lovely" said Jane

"My quarters are great," added Leon, "and Janine's studio is a magnificent space"

"Yes, when she's on a roll she sleeps down there, sometimes paints late into the night"

Just then Janine appeared with a tray of glasses, a big bowl of ice and a dusty green bottle,

"I thought you should try some of the local cider, we are famous for it here and we have pork for dinner so will be right I think, and a cup of tea for you Jane" she said

"Fantastic" said Davy

"Only one glass for you monsieur if you want wine with your dinner" she bent to kiss the top of his head

"So dinner in perhaps an hour?" she said and strolled back to the kitchen

The other three burst out laughing

" Rebel tamed eh Davy ?" said Leon

"Yes, well she's keeping me alive" he said ruefully

"Now, I have got a treat for us after dinner. You know Clare, Gideon's widow, is getting married again. I see her occasionally when I am in London , she's selling their house and a few months ago she gave me a box of stuff, she's been doing a massive clear out and this was all stuff from the 60's. Well there was lots of 16mm film, I don't think Gideon threw anything away, so I got an old chum of his at the BBC to have it looked at"

All three of his listeners were agog, wondering what he had found.

"I asked him specifically to check on our time, 66-69, everything was date labelled, I could see that when I checked the stuff and this bloke had it digitised and now I have it on a CD."

They all exclaimed with wonder and delight and maybe some trepidation. What would they see? They reminisced as to how, once Gideon had got his hands on a film camera, he used to randomly film, the house, rehearsals, people in the street, gigs, the sea front, mastering the equipment and by the time he and Marina had gone to Paris in May 68 he was confident and brimming with ideas.

Janine called them in and they sat down to a delicious dinner of

Andouille de Guemene, Janine explained how this was a Breton speciality served at village feasts, her version as well as the traditional sausage included herrings and warm potatoes. To follow she served a Tarte Tatin and they drank a delicious chilled white wine.

"Surpassed yourself Cherie" said Davy, finally heaving himself up from the table "But now let's go to the movies!"

"I will bring cheese into the salon, and maybe a Calvados, special treat Davy?"

Talking, thanking Janine and swapping reminiscences they followed Davy into a spacious room, next to the kitchen. There were two comfortable sofas, several assorted armchairs and of course paintings everywhere. Davy had already connected his computer to a large television screen.

Sarah said "How shall we do this? Shall we watch it straight through? Pause if something comes up"

Leon said "Maybe play it by ear but yes I think we might want to pause sometimes, pause for thought maybe?"

Jane stayed silent, wondering how she would feel to see their long-ago selves again.

Janine appeared with a board of Breton cheeses and the Calvados.

"Only small one for you Davy" she said and she quickly explained the selection of Breton cheeses on the board she had brought in ,Timanoix, Abbaye de Timadeuc and Saint Pulin

"Enough Janine" said Davy "She could talk about Breton cuisine forever" he laughed " We're gagging to see the film"

The others all agreed and helping themselves to calvados and a selection of cheese they all settled down. Sarah and Janine together on one sofa, Leon and Jane on the other and Davy next to his computer.

The first screen images were random, close ups on faces, tracking shots of the pier and beach in Brighton,

'Oh, that's the café" exclaimed Sarah, shots of brightly dressed people at tables, a close up on a huge Hendrix poster.

"Our clothes!" moaned Jane, "We look as if we are in fancy dress"

"We were of course" chuckled Davy, "God I loved my fringed leather jacket, wore it until it fell apart"

"Yeh, I remember that jacket" said Leon and then they were in the kitchen of St Agnes Avenue,

"Pause, pause" said Sarah.

There was the big table, covered in dirty cups, overflowing ashtrays, leaflets, cigarette papers, the image had paused on Davy rolling a spliff, Jane filling the kettle at the sink, Leon standing over by the oven, Paul with his legs flung cross the arms of his battered old armchair, Sarah at the table, her legs up on another chair.

"They all looked in silence then Sarah said

"I was thinking the other day the last time we all went to a funeral together it was Paul's, not you darling" she said to Jane

" You were too ill, but us and Gideon we were all together."

"I so wanted to be there but, but, it was too hard" Tears filled her eyes, Leon put an arm around her shoulder.

"Ah Cherie" said Janine reaching across, "that boy, Paul, he looked like an angel, perhaps he was meant to die young"

Sarah looked at her in surprise, Davy shrugged his shoulders

"She is a bit of a mystic" he said, smiling fondly at Janine.

Jane took a deep breath

"Play it again," she said . Now the scene was animated, the sound was poor but they could hear talk and laughter, music in the background, Gideon's voice telling them to look at the camera, Davy pulling a stupid face, Leon giving the finger, Sarah beaming, Paul staring straight at the camera

"Pause," said Jane. And then

"I really loved Paul, he was so kind and understanding."

She turned to Janine

"I was so stupid back then, I was ridiculously in love with Gideon, he was my first love but he was completely tied up with Marina. I was just a respite from her intensity, I understand that now, but then, I hoped he would be with me. And Paul really loved him too, we were foli a deux, and then I had the abortion and Gideon was so careless, Paul comforted me, gave me hope, foolish I know and then he died and I found him." She was finding it hard to talk, there were pauses whilst she drew shuddering breaths, Leon's arm tightened around her. " And I had a sort of breakdown"

Janine came to sit on her other side, patted her leg,

" And now you understand. That was how it was and you recovered and are happy now" '

" Yes , yes I am", and she glanced at Leon , " I am a different person from that silly deluded girl"

" Oh don't be hard on yourself ,we are all deluded when we are young. We think the world is ours for grabbing, that nothing can hurt us, life teaches different pretty quickly" said Davy.

" Let's see what's next"

"Yes sorry, but I feel I needed to get that off my chest. I'm ok now.' said Jane, she took a deep drink of her Calvados and turned to smile at Leon who squeezed her shoulder.

"No worries, so here we go" said Davy

The whole next bit was the Ranters, rehearsals, hanging about, the grubby old hall they used to meet. All of them exclaimed and laughed, talking over each other, Janine laughing loudest of all

"Davy your hair! Your moustache"

" God I don't remember I used to have a ponytail" groaned Leon, embarrassed by his past self. .

" Oh Jane, weren't we gorgeous" said Sarah and then there was an extended sequence, it was of Marina teaching one of the dance routines. They watched intently, Janine commenting on Marina's beauty and dominance.

"God yes, she was strict with us, think she had done dance at someplace, knew what she was doing" said Sarah

"She never really praised us though, if she said ok we were chuffed' remembered Jane.

"She is so impassive here" remarked Leon " Hard to tell what she's thinking'

"Yes' said Davy, "I never knew what she was thinking, she did not say much either"

" Hmm, what she did say was mainly bitchy" said Sarah

"Ah," said Janine "Now, I have read her book, it is easy to see she was a very unhappy person, felt deeply rejected and so she rejected others, what is the expression, lashed about"

" No love, lashed out," said Davy. "I told you Janine was reading her book, have we had enough now of this for now?" he asked " Janine could give us a bit of a summary of the book"

They all agreed, maybe they would watch more but for now they all wanted to know what revelations were in store about the enigmatic Marina.

" So I digest for you, I think maybe you are interested in her early years? But first I must say I liked her paintings. Her exhibition was very interesting, intense and quite angry work but later ones, like her book, calm, almost tranquil.

"I was intrigued about her upper class background, on both sides of the channel" said Leon " She kept that very quiet"

"O but we did then" said Sarah .

"'We all wanted to be working class, or classless"

"Hmph" said Davy, "cannot hide cultural capital though, guess that is where her arrogance stemmed from"

"Carry on Janine," said Jane, "What did you learn?"

" So, her parents had met in London during the war, her father was with the Free French and the mother was an interpreter she had been to finished school in Switzerland and was fluent"

" Finishing school" said Davy

. " Ah bien mais shh, they were young and in love, it was wartime and then Marina was born. Her maman was only 21, the war ended they went back to Paris and the maman discovered her dashing French man was a boring and conventional minor aristocrat and she wanted life and fun"

"Sounds like a book could be written about her" said Sarah

"Yes, well it seems Marina has reconciled with her but she was marrying many times, moving around. Marina was mainly in Paris but when her father married again she was sent off to English experimental schools"

" Progressive" said Davy

"oui , oui, and the new French family, more children, all very correct ,she did not fit in ,she was an ugly enfant"

"Marina? Ugly?" said Jane

"Yes, sulky sullen face,skinny, braces, mad hair, this is how she describes herself, but by the time you knew her the ugly duckling was a swan but still ugly inside "

"Oh dear, I feel sorry for her, she must have felt that Sarah and I were from a different planet"said Jane

"Yes" said Sarah thoughtfully 'we were loved, secure, could spread our wings because we felt safe" said Sarah

" When I met her in India, in 72 and she was in such a state, from the things she said I sensed a lot of this , that her arrogance and disdain hid a massive hurt" said Leon.

They were all silent for a minute, each of them rearranging in their minds the Marina they had known.

" She talks a bit in her book about Brighton, but mainly about this older man, her professor? Teacher? That she was having an affairre with" Janine continued .

" What? " said Sarah and Jane in unison .

"He was married, had small children, maybe a father figure, it dragged on for a couple of years, all very secret but she says that she loved him and had a musician boyfriend to make him jealous and to make herself feel better"

" A revelation eh? " said Davy .

" When Janine told me about him it explained a few oddities. I think Gideon knew about him. Gideon used Marina, you know, for her contacts, her money, you remember she always had plenty of money, she would pay when they went to Paris and when they went to California. He told me that"

"Oh" said Sarah " it is like a kaleidoscope, everything is rearranged"

Jane was thoughtful

" Do you remember Sarah , a couple of times there was an older good looking guy came to gigs and Marina would go to the back and talk to him in the break?"

 She had always been conscious of what Marina was doing, if she was with Gideon or at the bar with her many admirers and those unusual times had resurfaced now.

"Hmm, I don't know," said Sarah. Jane thought about what Davy had said, maybe Gideon had always known and did not care .

 "In the rest of the book she talks about the summer of love in San Francisco, going to India , she does mention meeting you Leon and how you helped her, and then there is a lot about her life in the Warhol entourage, he had an apartment in Paris you know, they met when she was studying at the Beaux Artes"

"ah, I had suggested she go back to art school," said Leon.

"And then it is less interesting, the bad wild times always more fun to read about" said Janine

"yeh , and to live until you get old," said Davy ruefully. Janine gave him a gentle punch and continued

"She met a woman, had therapy, became a lesbian and now is in peace. Voila" finished Janine.

Silence then Sarah said "I hope it is translated into English, I would like to read it.I wonder what would it be like to see her again, knowing all this?"

" I have no desire to, we can all think about her differently but life is too short to meet people you disliked 40 years ago" said Leon firmly. Jane looked at him, then said thoughtfully

"No,I don't want to see her but I am glad to understand her better, and anyway she might not even remember us, her life sounds to have been incredibly full" she said a trifle wistfully.

" yes I am sure you are right" said Sarah "what do you think Davy?" Davy was remembering those unexpected and passionate nights he had had with Marina, but looking at his dear comfortable Janine on the sofa he slowly shook his head,

 Nope, the past is another country and I've lost my bloody passport" They all laughed, Janine bustled out to the kitchen to make tea and coffee, Davy put the DVD on again and they watched random scenes, laughing and commenting, there was a feeling of catharsis in the air, they all felt it, the past had finally been laid to rest .

Printed in Great Britain
by Amazon